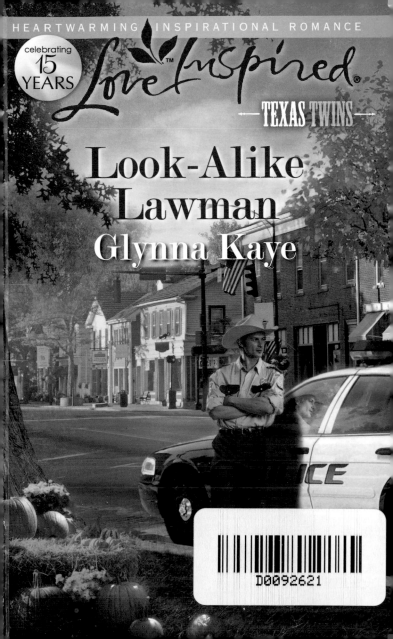

HEARTWARMING INSPIRATIONAL ROMANCE

celebrating
15
YEARS

Love Inspired®

← TEXAS TWINS →

Look-Alike
Lawman

Glynna Kaye

D0092621

INSPIRATIONAL

Love Inspired®

celebrating
15
YEARS

Contemporary inspirational romances with Christian characters
facing the challenges of life and love in today's world.

ISBN-13:978-0-373-87770-6

EAN

LIATMIFC1012

"Thank you again for going out of your way for my son," Elise said. "But he needs to get to his homework and I need to get back to my job."

Gray smiled down at the boy. "Can't slack on the homework, mister. Wannabe police officers have to keep up their grades."

The child groaned, then lifted a hand for a parting high five before trotting back to the house.

The officer turned to her, his probing gaze setting loose a truckload of battering rams in her stomach.

For a moment she thought Cory's cop was going to say something else. But he merely motioned to her vehicle at the curb. "I'd better let you get on your way."

She was unwilling to get too chatty with the more-than-attractive man. No, he hadn't crossed the lines of propriety as some had done. Hadn't asked her out. Nevertheless, she kept up her guard.

* * *

**Texas Twins: Two sets of twins,
torn apart by family secrets, find their way home.**

Books by Glynna Kaye

Love Inspired

Dreaming of Home
Second Chance Courtship
At Home in His Heart
High Country Hearts
Look-Alike Lawman

GLYNNA KAYE

treasures memories of growing up in small midwestern towns—in Iowa, Missouri, Illinois—and vacations spent in another rural community with the Texan side of the family. She traces her love of storytelling to the many times a houseful of great-aunts and great-uncles gathered with her grandma to share hours of what they called "windjammers"—candid, heartwarming, poignant and often humorous tales of their youth and young adulthood.

Glynna now lives in Arizona, and when she isn't writing she's gardening and enjoying photography and the great outdoors.

Look-Alike Lawman

Glynna Kaye

Love Inspired

Special thanks and acknowledgment to Glynna Kaye
for her contribution to the Texas Twins miniseries.

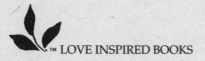

™ LOVE INSPIRED BOOKS

PLEASE RECYCLE
THIS PRODUCT IS RECYCLABLE

Recycling programs
for this product may
not exist in your area.

ISBN-13: 978-0-373-87770-6

LOOK-ALIKE LAWMAN

Copyright © 2012 by Harlequin Books S.A.

Trust in the Lord with all your heart
and lean not on your own understanding;
in all your ways acknowledge him
and he will make your paths straight.
—*Proverbs* 3:5,6

To my wonderful Love Inspired editors:
Melissa Endlich, Emily Rodmell and Rachel Burkot.
Thank you for believing in me!

Chapter One

"My daddy was a policeman, too. A bad guy killed him."

Grayson Wallace stared at the boy gazing up at him. The little chin jutted in evident pride, but the dark brown eyes searched his own for understanding. A connection. Acknowledgment. He was only a first-grader, not too much older than the son of Gray's former girlfriend. Way too young to have lost his daddy, let alone lost him to a bad guy.

Gray massaged the shoulder of his own left arm, which was held close to his body in a sling. Hadn't the division captain said, when asking for a volunteer, that visiting a Fort Worth elementary school's career day was cushy duty? He could still hear the good-natured hoots and catcalls of his fellow officers when he'd raised his hand. Couldn't blame them. He didn't have kids of his own. Spent almost every waking moment trying to keep lowlifes off the streets. He wasn't known for coaching T-ball, catching Disney matinees or reading bedtime stories in his spare time like many of the other guys and gals did.

But then, they weren't aware of how close he'd let himself get to Jenna's boy.

No, catering to kids might not be his gift, but hanging out with grade-schoolers for a few hours was better than another day sitting around the office shuffling paperwork as he'd done the past several weeks. This was a perfect task for a cop on limited duty, recovering from a shoulder injury sustained during an undercover assignment.

But now, looking into this child's pain-filled eyes, it sure didn't strike him as *cushy*.

Grayson crouched in front of the dark-haired boy, aware of other kids crowding close, and uttered the words he instinctively knew the youngster needed to hear. "It takes a lot of courage to be the son of a law-enforcement officer."

The boy blinked back tears and nodded, his eyes reflecting gratitude that Grayson had taken notice of him.

Poor kid.

"What's your name?"

"Cory Lopez, sir."

Sir. Didn't hear that a lot these days, even in the South. Gray held out his hand and clasped the small one offered. Gave it a man-to-man shake. "Good to meet you, Cory. Like your teacher said earlier, I'm Officer Grayson Wallace."

The first-grader took a deep breath. "My dad is Duke Lopez. Did you know him?"

Cory's gaze held steady in confident expectation.

Duke Lopez. Gray remembered the name, although he'd never met him. Lopez hadn't been one of Fort Worth's finest, but on a force in one of the outlying communities. Nevertheless, any time a cop went down in the line of duty, you knew about it. It impacted you. You never forgot.

"No, I didn't know him, Cory." The hope in the boy's eyes dimmed, and Gray almost regretted admitting the truth. "But he was a brave man. I heard how he saved his partner."

The boy took a step closer. "He was a hero."

"Yes, he was."

"When I grow up, I'm going to be a policeman hero, too."

Gray flinched inwardly. His mother must love that. "That's a fine thing to aspire to, Cory."

"I'm going to be a firefighter," a dainty African-American girl piped up, easing shyly closer to Gray. Like Cory, her outfit conformed to one of the acceptable variations of the Fort Worth Independent School District's K-8 dress code—a collared navy shirt and khaki pants. The regulations helped keep kids from all walks of life on more even footing starting out and served to discourage gang affiliation and too-provocative clothing.

"A firefighter is a fine thing to be, too."

The girl beamed and nudged a classmate.

"Did a bad guy hurt you, mister?" A blond boy pointed at Gray's sling. Did he dare admit to kids this young that there were not-so-nice people in the world? Then again, in this neighborhood, that was nothing they didn't already know.

And Cory knew it for sure.

"Okay, children." Miss Gilbert clapped her hands to get the attention of the first-graders, her cheerful voice raised over the childish chatter. "Time to clean up."

Gray glanced at the clock. He'd already been at the school several hours, rotating through the elementary classroom along with a fireman, doctor, veterinarian and a marine like his little brother Carter. Each told about what they did and answered eager—and sometimes amusing—questions. But it was now two forty-five on a Friday afternoon. He needed to get going. He had to report back at Division, then pack a few things and head out for a five-hour drive to a western Texas community called Grasslands.

While he'd gone there for the first time only last weekend, he'd delayed that particular trip for weeks. With his injuries to be attended to and post-assignment paperwork and court appearances filling in time until the end of September, he'd had a legitimate excuse for staying away. But truth be known, he'd needed time to digest his little sister Maddie's news—that while he'd been away on the undercover assignment, she'd discovered they had family they hadn't known existed.

She had a twin sister, Violet, and he an identical twin brother. He still wouldn't believe it if he hadn't come face-to-face with Jack Colby only a handful of days ago in a Grasslands church parking lot. The revelation that Sharla Wallace, the only mother he'd ever known, wasn't his and Maddie's birth mother compounded the shock. And he still hadn't gotten his head around the fact that a woman named Belle Colby—Jack and Violet's mother—was his and Maddie's biological mother, as well.

But Belle was in a coma sustained from injuries when she'd fallen from a horse last summer. Which is why he'd agreed to return to the Colby Ranch this first weekend in October. There were things he and his newfound siblings needed to work through together, decisions to be made. This next trip wasn't one he looked forward to any more than he had the first one.

"Children! I said it's time to clean up."

Gray stood, and the kids eagerly scattered to their workstations. All except Cory, who continued to gaze at him with what could only be described as a reverential look. Not good. Gray motioned to the other kids. "I think you're supposed to get your stuff and catch a bus home or something."

"My mom picks me up."

"Then you'll want to be ready when she gets here."

"She's always late."

They stared at each other in silence. What did the kid want from him? He'd already told him he didn't know his father, but he could feel the boy's pain. His longing. While he hadn't been an orphan himself, he knew what it was like to grow up without a mom. His mother—or at least the woman he had thought was his mother—had died in a car accident when he was not much older than Cory, so he knew the loss of a parent he'd loved.

He knew, too, what it was like to miss his dad. He had no idea where his missionary-doctor father might be. Gray had returned from last month's close-call, determined to strengthen his relationship with his dad. But Brian Wallace had been reported as ill somewhere along the Texas-Mexico border and all efforts to trace him during recent weeks had been unsuccessful. No, Gray's situation wasn't exactly like Cory's, but it nevertheless tugged at his heart.

"Can I touch your badge?"

Jerked back to the present, Gray couldn't help but smile at the innocent request. What would it hurt? He squatted again and the boy tentatively reached out a finger to the panther crouched atop the shield. Symbol of Panther City, a nickname for Fort Worth since the late 1800s.

"He looks mean," Cory whispered, stroking the big cat almost as if he could feel the animal's thick, muscled coat under his fingertip.

"He does, doesn't he?"

"Like he could eat bad guys."

Gray drew a sharp breath. It had been two years since Duke Lopez had taken a bullet while drawing a gunman's attention from his fallen partner. Cory would have been, what? Four? How well did he remember his father?

"Cory, your mom is here," Miss Gilbert called from the doorway. "I see her coming down the hall."

Good. The little guy's mother wasn't late after all.

The boy's eyes reflected evident surprise at her on-time arrival, then he gave the panther a final pat. Their gazes met in solemn recognition of a mutual bond that caught Gray off guard.

"It's an honor to meet the son of Duke Lopez."

The boy nodded, then in a flash scampered to his workstation to clean up and gather his things. Gray rose and turned, preparing to give the boy's mother a courteous nod. But his smile froze. *Whoa.* That was the kid's mother? Since when did moms look like that?

Even in profile as she stood chatting in the doorway with

Miss Gilbert, she was a beauty. Dark flashing eyes. Dazzling smile. A warm, flawlessly creamy Hispanic skin tone. Shiny black hair pulled into a demure bun contrasted with the spiky heels, short skirt and a molded-to-her-figure blazer.

Cory hoisted his backpack over his shoulder and raced to the door, breathlessly pointing toward Gray.

"Mom! A policeman! And he knows Daddy is a hero."

She turned startled eyes toward him—and the open, friendly expression evaporated from her striking features. Her lustrous brown eyes locked on his for a long moment before narrowing slightly. She then put a protective arm around her son's shoulders and ushered him from the room.

"But Mom," Cory protested for at least the tenth time since leaving the elementary school. "I wanted you to meet Officer Wallace. He doesn't know Daddy, but he remembers him. He knows he saved his partner. Don't you even care?"

"Of course I care." Elise Lopez attempted to keep her voice even, not wanting Cory to sense how upsetting his growing obsession with policemen had become for her. Her hands tightened on the steering wheel as she parked her compact car in front of the tiny fourplex they'd called home for the past year and a half. Far from being the most fashionable of the city's districts—it bordered on rough—it was all she could afford right now. Close to school and her job at the clinic.

"Then why didn't you talk to him?"

"Now, Cory, you know I never have time to chat when I pick you up. Billie Jean is expecting you and I've got to get back to work."

His shoulders slumped. "You always have to get back to work."

"I know." Hearing his sigh as they exited the vehicle and headed across the sparsely grassed, hard-packed sand yard, she thrust aside memories of the well-cared-for landscape of their former home. She placed a hand on her young son's shoulder. "But I go to work because *te amo. Sí?*"

I love you.

And she did, with every breath she'd taken since she'd first suspected she was pregnant. She'd held him even closer to her heart since his father's murder two summers ago. Duke. Her hero, whom she'd learned not long after his death had more than a bit of tarnish smudging his shining armor.

But there was no point in rehashing that and making herself miserable. It was what it was. She could never have foreseen how his gambling debts would come back to haunt her, draining his life insurance and their savings and leaving her and Cory in dire circumstances that they had yet to dig out of. But Duke had otherwise been a good man. A loving father. A courageous cop.

"Oh, man." Cory's groan startled her as he jerked to a halt and dropped to his knees, frantically searching through his backpack. "Oh, man."

"What's wrong?"

"I left my ball glove at school." The glove his father had given him. He looked up at her, his dark eyes reflecting panic. "We've got to go back and get it, Mom. Someone might steal it."

She looked at her watch, torn. Why did he always do this to her? Forgetting things she'd reminded him about a million times. She'd even warned him that very morning not to take the baseball glove to school, but he'd apparently sneaked it into his pack.

"There's no time. I'll be late getting back to work again."

"Oh, man." But Cory didn't cry or beg as he might have several months ago. Instead, he cut her a dirty look, snatched up his backpack and raced ahead of her into the open door of the fourplex's miniscule entryway.

Her stomach knotted. That baseball glove meant the world to him, but she couldn't go back to hunt it down. Last month a coworker had been let go for being late. Like Elise, she was a single mom juggling the logistics of a full-time job and kids, but chronic tardiness and absenteeism at the clinic hadn't been tolerated for long.

With a glance at the potted pink geranium she'd set on the front step last spring—a pitiful remnant of her former lush gardens—she followed her son into the building, passing the lockboxes where residents received mail. All except her. She had a post-office box elsewhere, ensuring no friends or family members could search for her street address online and learn the truth about the neighborhood where she now resided.

Slowly she climbed the threadbare carpeted steps to their second-story apartment, a sparsely furnished space unlike any she'd ever imagined living in.

Yes, Duke had been a courageous cop. But his surreptitious penchant for playing the ponies had been his—and her—downfall.

Which brought her back to Cory's fascination with policemen—like the well-built, good-looking guy at the school that afternoon. All spit-shined and polished in an official black uniform for his career day appearance, his dark chestnut hair neatly clipped, he exuded that quintessential cop aura. Confident. Authoritative. A bit cocky.

And a proud Texan.

She could see it all there in the flashing seconds when he'd held her gaze. He hadn't even had the courtesy to cloak his appreciative glance as it fleetingly swept over her, his expressive eyes questioning if she returned his interest.

Which she did not.

She'd never again willingly put herself in a position to wait up late at night, anxiously listening for the garage door to signal the safe return of her hero. There would be no more haunting reminders, when embraced in the arms of a body armor-clad man, that the bulletproof vest was there for a reason. No heart-stopping moments when an unidentified police officer was reported as injured on the 5 o'clock news. She'd never again risk the nightmare of two somber officers at the door in the dead of the night, waiting to take her to the hospital. Or endure the heartbreak of not getting there in time to say goodbye.

No, never again. She hoped she'd made that plain enough when she broke visual contact with Cory's Officer Wallace and hurried her son from the building.

"Mom?" His face still a thundercloud as he waited at the apartment door, Cory jerked past her when she let them inside. "How old do you have to be before you can be a policeman?"

The cop thing again. But at least he was speaking to her. "Much older than you are now."

"How old?"

"Depends. Twenty-one, usually." Twenty-one. That's how old Duke had been when he'd moved to Texas where his bilingual fluency and three years of law-enforcement coursework were much sought after.

He hadn't lived but a week beyond twenty-six.

Three years her senior, he'd been her childhood sweetheart in their small Arizona hometown. Which was why she couldn't move back there, no matter how much she wanted to. Not yet. Not until she could return with her head held high, her finances restored and the weakness of Tomas "Duke" Lopez well-hidden from family and the community.

Cory flung his backpack to the hardwood floor and flopped onto the worn couch of the diminutive living room. Then, as if coming to a sudden conclusion, he scrambled to the sole end table, opened a drawer and pulled out the massive city phone book.

His reading skills were rapidly progressing, but he still had a considerable way to go. Nevertheless, he determinedly flipped through the thin-sheeted pages as she speed-dialed his sitter, their downstairs neighbor Billie Jean.

"Change out of your school clothes, Cory. Don't dawdle."

She glanced impatiently at her watch. It was disruptive enough to her employer that they'd accommodated her taking a midafternoon lunch hour each day. Even with the school situated between home and work, when traffic was congested there wasn't much wiggle room to pick up Cory, deposit him at Billie Jean's and get back to the clinic.

"Mom?"

As she waited for her friend to answer, she turned to her son, who still lingered over the phone directory spread across his lap.

"Yes?"

"I've got to get my ball glove back, so I need the help of a policeman. How do you spell *Wallace?*"

"Thank you again for coming." Miss Gilbert, an attractive blonde in her early twenties, smiled at Grayson. "You and the other professionals made quite a positive impression on my class. On the whole school, in fact. But especially on Cory Lopez."

"Cute kid." *With a gorgeous but stuck-up mom.* "Too bad about his dad."

"Yes. The sudden loss continues to take its toll, as is apparent from his behavior."

"His behavior?"

"According to his former kindergarten teacher, it's been like night and day compared to last year. Restless and distracted. Playing rough. Aggressive. Almost obsessed with following in his father's footsteps and getting even with the man who shot him."

Grayson frowned. "They have the guy in jail. I know it's not been the customary swift Texas justice, but he's awaiting trial."

"That doesn't mean much to a little boy."

"No, I imagine not."

"I couldn't help but notice, though, how he settled down almost from the moment you arrived. Do you have children of your own, Mr. Wallace?" Her quick glance took in his left hand prominently supported by the sling, then her smooth cheeks flushed. He smiled to himself. Checking him out for a ring, was she?

"No, no kids," he admitted. But maybe on down the road.

"Must be the uniform, then. Reminded him of his father."

"Could be."

"He's a child with so much potential. Elise—his mother—works hard to provide for him, to give him love and attention. But a troubled boy that age could use a strong male influence. Have you ever thought about our district's mentoring program?"

"What's that?" If it was what he thought it was, he wanted no part of it. He didn't intend to get attached to anyone else's kid ever again.

"It's an opportunity to connect with children in a meaningful way. Too many in this part of town come from broken homes that are struggling financially. There are few good role models." She lifted her gaze to his in appeal. "I'd love to see a youngster like Cory have a chance, not end up like so many drawn to street gangs in order to find a place where they feel they belong."

"I doubt I'd be much of a mentor for a first-grader. Maybe an older boy, if I had the time. Which I don't."

"At least please give it some thought, Mr. Wallace." Her cheeks flushed again. "I'm sure you noticed how the children—Cory—gravitated to you."

Yeah, he'd noticed how Cory had sidled up to him, especially when he'd crouched to his level. How the boy had moved in close, basking in the attention. Jenna's son had been the same. He and Michael had been drawn to each other.

Grown close. Closer than Gray had ever been to a little kid. Did Michael understand why Gray was no longer a part of his life? Did Jenna explain it to him at all?

He shoved away the haunting speculation. "Cory's a friendly little guy."

"I know it's your job to keep the 'bad guys' at bay, Mr. Wallace, but what if those bad guys had once had a man in their lives who cared about what happened to them?" Miss Gilbert's smile again encouraged, but it would get her nowhere.

His memory flew to his brother who'd been raised without a father when their parents had split and each took two kids. Jack turned out okay, didn't he? Then again, he'd grown up on a ranch, not in the heart of a big city.

"I don't mean to pressure you," the teacher amended, apparently mistaking his silence for annoyance. "But I've come to love Cory. A policeman like you, who's already had a thorough background check, could move quickly through the mentor screening process."

"Thank you for putting confidence in me, Miss Gilbert, but I'm afraid it isn't feasible right now."

"I understand."

Sensing her disappointment, he realized it was time he drew the conversation to a close. "I'd better gather my own things and be on my way. Let you finish up and get started on your weekend."

He shook her hand, then crossed the room to retrieve the box of "cop props" he'd brought to show the kids. He paused to pick up a baseball glove that had been kicked under a nearby table, but when he turned to give it to Miss Gilbert, she was no longer in the room.

He glanced down at the kid-size glove in his hand and smiled. He still had his own junior-size one stashed in a box in his closet. The kid who'd left this one behind wouldn't sleep a wink all weekend not knowing until Monday if it was safe. Memories of the years he and his younger sister and brother had lived in rural Appleton flooded back. Of the times after the woman he knew as Mom died and Dad returned them all to the city and became immersed in medical school. Times when the highlight of his day was when his dad tossed a few balls with him before burying himself in his textbooks.

Gray thoughtfully turned the glove in his hands, noticing a name printed on it with a black felt-tip marker.

C. Lopez.

Cory, whose dad had died in an attempt to serve and protect. He started to toss the glove to a nearby table, but something on the inside edge caught his eye. A label. *Cornelio Tomas Lopez.*

And a street address.

The boy's eyes, hungering for reassurance, pierced Gray's memory—followed by the remembrance of the flashing gaze of his beautiful, standoffish mother.

Miss Gilbert said Cory's mom loved him. That she did her best to provide for him and give him the attention he needed. He knew from his experiences with Jenna and Michael, though, that it wasn't easy being a single mom raising a boy on your own.

He tightened his grip on the ball glove, his gaze lingering on the inner label.

No, don't even think about it, Wallace.

Chapter Two

She'd just stepped out the front door when an unfamiliar silver SUV pulled up at the curb behind her car.

Cory's Officer Wallace got out.

Elise's grip tightened on her car keys. What was he doing here? How did he know where she lived? Surely Miss Gilbert wouldn't share her address with a flirtatious *cop* of all people. If he'd followed her home to hit on her, he could climb back into his vehicle and head on down the road.

"Mrs. Lopez?" a warm, masculine Texas twang called out as he rounded the SUV and approached. His gaze swept the apartment house and yard in one of those looks she knew quickly—and accurately—assessed the neighborhood. These were her circumstances…and he clearly found them lacking. But his smile nevertheless broadened as he held up something in the hand unfettered by a sling. A baseball glove. "Cory forgot this."

Thoughtful on the surface, but why had he made such an effort to deliver it personally unless he had an ulterior motive? She gave him an uncertain smile as he came to stand before her. He was taller than she'd originally thought, with a strong, clean-shaven jaw. High cheekbones. Straight nose. His confident, captivating eyes were an unusual light brown, like burnished oak edged with a darker shade. Thick, dark lashes.

Eyes a woman could too easily get lost in.

Nor had she missed that the hand extending from the sling's edge was ringless—although it wasn't uncommon for cops on duty not to wear one.

"I'm Grayson Wallace, ma'am. I visited the elementary school today. Met your son."

As if Cory would let her forget. Or if she could forget her brief, disconcerting encounter with the handsome lawman. "Good afternoon, Officer Wallace. This is a surprise."

"I imagine so." Lines crinkled around the corners of his eyes as he undoubtedly recognized the suspicion in her own—telltale lines that signaled this was a man who liked to laugh. Who enjoyed good times. "I didn't want him to go all weekend without his ball glove. I know when I was his age, I'd have gone crazy if I'd thought I'd lost mine."

He held out the leather glove, his gaze never leaving hers, but she mishandled the exchange and it slipped from her fingers. His hand brushed hers as he deftly caught it.

"Sorry, ma'am. My fault."

His gaze trapped hers once more as he again handed it to her. She tucked the glove securely under her arm, then brushed back a strand of hair straying from her chignon. She'd dealt with plenty of men who'd tried to overstep their bounds since Duke's death. Returning a beloved baseball glove was one more creative ploy to get a foot in the door of her personal life. She could send this one packing, too.

"Thank you. Cory didn't notice it was missing until we got home. Pretty upset. He wanted to call a policeman to retrieve it because I didn't have time to go back." *Any excuse to see his Officer Wallace again.*

"So it is a special glove." The smiling eyes sobered. "His father gave it to him?"

Perceptive man.

She nodded. "For his fourth birthday. A few weeks be-fore…"

Her gaze faltered as her voice drifted off. Some days it was still hard to talk about. Especially uncomfortable to discuss with another police officer.

"I'm sorry for your loss, Mrs. Lopez." He studied her with a sincere respect, any hint of flirtatiousness extinguished. "I never met your husband, but I knew of him. He was a fine officer."

"Thank you. He was."

He broke eye contact. Like many others, he no doubt found it difficult to talk to the widow of a fallen comrade. What can you say that hadn't already been said? Besides, what cop wanted an in-your-face reminder that some police officers, like soldiers, never come home?

"Officer Wallace! What are you doing here?"

She turned to see Cory dash out the front door, eyes aglow with curiosity and excitement. He jerked to a halt beside her, an eager gaze fastened on their visitor.

"He brought you this." She reluctantly handed him his baseball glove, not thrilled to elevate the police officer any higher in her son's estimation than he already was.

"Oh, man. Oh, man." Cory thrust his hand into the glove, mixed emotions warring in his eyes. He took a step toward the uniformed man, hesitated, then moved in closer to wrap his arms around the startled officer for a hug. "Oh, man, thank you. I thought someone would steal it."

Officer Wallace's hearty laugh rang out as he returned the enthusiastic embrace, his gaze flickering to hers and hold-ing it longer than necessary. "You're welcome, Cory. I know what a favorite glove can mean to a guy."

Flustered, she glanced at her watch. "Thank you again for going out of your way for Cory. But he needs to get to his homework, and I need to get back to my job."

He smiled down at her son. "Can't slack on the homework, mister. Wannabe police officers have to keep up their grades."

Cory groaned, then lifted a hand for a parting high five before trotting back to the house, the glove held high in triumph.

Still smiling, the officer turned to her, his probing gaze setting loose a truckload of battering rams in her stomach.

"You've got a good kid there."

She shot him a grateful look. "Most of the time. He's had his moments lately."

"It's not easy on a boy, losing his father."

"No." Nor was losing a husband easy. Or discovering he wasn't who you'd believed him to be. "I don't mean to sound ungrateful, Mr. Wallace, but if you visit the school again I'd appreciate your not indulging his obsession about becoming a policeman. He talks about it nonstop. It's not healthy for him."

Or for me.

He squinted one eye and offered a hint of a smile. He probably thought her overly protective. "I wouldn't worry too much about that, ma'am. He's six, right? Today he wants to be a lawman. Tomorrow it will be a veterinarian. Or an astronaut. Or a cowboy."

"I can hope—and pray—that's so."

For a moment she thought Cory's cop was going to say something else. Make an observation. Ask a question. But he merely motioned to her vehicle at the curb. "I'd better let you get on your way."

"I am cutting it close. Can't afford to be late." With a polite but dismissive nod, she moved toward her car. To her dismay, he kept up with her stride for stride.

"Where do you work?"

"Not too far from here. At a medical clinic down the street from that big used-car dealership. You know the one?"

"I do. So, you're a nurse? Therapist?"

She noticed he didn't ask if she was a doctor—the neighborhood alone answered that question easily enough. But the assumption that she'd have a degree beyond high school stung. Becoming a physical therapist had long been her dream. But Cory had arrived shy of a year of marriage and Duke had insisted that education take a backseat until the kids—however many came along—were in school.

"No. I'm a receptionist, medical records manager and general go-to gal."

"So on your feet all day." A smile tugged as he glanced down at her strappy, high-heeled sandals, the wisdom of which his amused expression questioned.

"Right." She took a slow breath as she reached her vehicle, unwilling to get too chatty with the undeniably attractive man. No, he hadn't crossed the lines of propriety as a few had done. He hadn't boldly hinted that a woman alone might appreciate some male companionship. He hadn't asked her out. Nevertheless, she kept up her guard. "Thank you again, Officer Wallace, for making a little boy very happy."

"The name's Grayson. Or Gray." He held out his hand.

"Elise," she offered reluctantly, as his big hand swallowed hers. She didn't want to be on a first-name basis with this cop.

"Pretty name."

"Thank you."

He released her hand, his brown eyes again questioning—as if still attempting to gauge the level of her interest. She braced herself, preparing to share too-often-practiced words to decline coffee. Dinner. Dessert. Or other more presumptuous propositions.

But to her surprise he merely fished momentarily in his uniform shirt pocket, then handed her a business card. Was this the latest strategy in the dating game realm? He thought he'd made a good enough impression that she'd call him?

Arrogant man.

He stepped back. "Good to meet you, Elise—and Cory as well. Hope you both have a great weekend."

With an absurd prick of disappointment, she watched him stroll to his SUV and climb in, lift his unencumbered hand in a parting gesture and drive away.

She glanced down at the business card and shook her head. Talk about egotistical. But he did have beautiful eyes and was polite.

And speaking of polite, where had *her* manners gotten off to? He'd gone out of his way to bring the baseball glove and she hadn't thought to ask how he'd injured his arm. How long he'd been in law enforcement.

Or if she would ever see him again.

Grayson pulled up in front of the Colby Ranch's sprawling main house just short of midnight. With considerable effort, he shoved aside the nagging thoughts of Elise Lopez and her son that had followed him as each mile stretched westward from Fort Worth. He could admit that if it weren't for the romantic debacle with Jenna months ago and the severed relationship with her son, he could see himself being drawn to the attractive single mom. Maybe even offering to mentor Cory. But he'd been burned. Badly. Did Jenna's boy feel the void of his abrupt departure as deeply as he did?

He turned off the ignition and, still gripping the steering wheel, sat staring at the two-story brick home, a few of its windows faintly aglow even at this late hour. The distinctive sweet, dry scent of western Texas wafted through his rolled-down window. The occasional low of distant cattle teased his city-accustomed ears, reminding him of his earliest boyhood years in another small rural town.

Had it been only a month since he'd returned from his undercover assignment to emails and frantic phone messages from his sister? He'd thought she'd lost her mind—Dad missing, a biological mother deep in a coma and an identical twin for both him and Maddie. But one look at their twins last weekend had settled any doubt about the blood connection.

They were kin, all right. Maddie's wild stories were true, but unfortunately Dad hadn't been located despite his and his siblings' best efforts.

"Lord," he whispered, absently massaging his injured shoulder, "you've gotta help me out here. Every fiber of my body wants to head straight back to Fort Worth. I don't want to deal with this."

He squared his shoulders as he exited the SUV and stretched his stiff legs. His newfound family was counting on him to locate Dad and find answers to the thousand and one questions they all had about their heritage. Questions no one but Dad or the woman going by the name Belle Colby could answer.

But that was another worm in the apple. Belle—he couldn't bring himself to think of her as "Mom"—lay unconscious at Ranchland Manor, a care facility a few miles away in Grasslands.

Having retrieved his duffel bag from the backseat, he'd barely headed toward the house when Maddie, Violet and Jack stepped onto the front porch to offer a warm welcome. All they needed was their baby brother, Carter—a marine on overseas deployment and still unaware of all the family drama—to make their homecoming complete.

"Grayson!" Maddie's breathless voice warmed him as he approached. His city-gal sis sure had taken to the country life since she and Violet had stumbled across each other in Fort Worth last July. A God-engineered coincidence for sure. "We were starting to get worried. Thought you'd never get here."

"Got a late start." No point in telling his nosy sister that a beautiful woman had been the cause. He'd never get a moment's peace.

Under the dim porch light, his brother Jack hung back, snatching uncomfortable glances in his direction as Violet and Maddie—both mindful of the sling—enveloped Gray in exuberant hugs. Jack's hair was longer than his, grazing the collar of a Western-cut shirt, and it appeared he didn't keep at that pesky five o'clock shadow as diligently as did his cop brother.

Clear, too, that he and Jack still shared an awkwardness despite efforts to get beyond the unnerving situation last weekend when they'd first met. Maddie and Violet didn't seem to have that problem. You'd have thought they'd grown up together. They even had similar mannerisms and could finish each other's sentences.

But he and Jack, while polite and friendly enough on the surface, were strangers. On guard. Uncomfortable with the whole situation.

When the sisters' lively welcome calmed down, Gray's twin thrust out his hand. "Good to have you back."

"Good to be back."

But from the wary look in Jack's eyes it was apparent he, too, recognized both were parroting expected pleasantries.

Inside the house Gray again sensed, as he had at his first visit, an emptiness in the home of his birth mother. He could detect a subdued, almost reverential hush in a place he'd been told that a few months ago she'd filled with love and laughter. It was evident, too, that Jack and Violet were out of their element in her absence and grieving her tragic situation.

Out of a sense of obligation—and curiosity—he'd joined his siblings in a visit to Belle at the Grasslands care facility last weekend. It had been another surreal moment as he'd stared down at a still-beautiful woman in her early forties, auburn hair spread across a pristine white pillow.

He'd been denied the opportunity to know the woman who'd cradled him and his twin side by side in her womb for nine months, who had given birth to them so many years ago.

Why?

From all he'd picked up on since the revelation of the family's state of affairs, she loved Jack and Violet with all her heart. Treasured them. Had she not felt the same way about him and Maddie? How could a mother choose between children?

"Gray?" Jerked from his inadvertent reverie, he turned to Maddie as they entered a spacious, warmly lit kitchen. "Kendra—I mean, Keira—and I are bunking together in the same room, so you can have mine like last weekend."

Keira was Jack's fiancée, a savvy blonde who'd landed on the Colbys' doorstep last month after a car accident left her without memory. They'd called her Kendra since she didn't have any ID on her. Thankfully, her memory eventually returned and they'd learned her real name was Keira Wolfe and she was a veterinarian. Jack had promptly staked his claim.

"I don't want to keep putting you ladies out." It was a five-bedroom place, but the master suite—Belle's—remained unoccupied. "The couch in the den would suit me fine."

His sisters made identical sounds of protest.

"It's just for tonight." Violet linked her arm through his uninjured one and once again he found himself staring in disbelief at her very existence. She looked amazingly like her twin, but with a country freshness all her own. A sprinkling of freckles. Auburn hair caught up in a long ponytail, she exuded a comfortable confidence no doubt born of a lifetime of ranching. "Jack's moving out to his new place tomorrow."

Jack had taken on a seventy-year-old house known to locals as the old Lindley place, the spread it sat on now part of the Colby Ranch.

He glanced at his brother. "That a fact? I imagine you're considerably more motivated to complete that renovation than you might have been a month ago."

Jack's eyes lit up and he offered his first grin. "A little lady will do that to a man. Get ready, Grayson. Your time's coming."

"Don't know about that." He ducked his head, wary that his perceptive sis might read his mind—pick up on an image of the beautiful Elise who'd filled his thoughts in recent hours. "I'm kind of attached to a bachelor life."

"Oh, Gray," Maddie blurted, placing her hands on her hips, "you're still wallowing in the after-effects of that breakup. Give yourself time."

He shot her a warning look. He didn't want to discuss his old girlfriend tonight. Certainly not in front of his newfound siblings—although he suspected from the way Violet nodded knowingly that Maddie had already filled her in. Dealing with one sister was challenging enough. Now he had two.

"Jack's been there, done that." Violet looked to their brother for confirmation. "He was crazy about a gal before she dumped him. But now that Keira's come along, he can barely remember Tammy's name. God knows what He's doing, Gray. He closes one door and opens another."

Gray managed a smile in Jack's direction, figuring he didn't much care for the sharing of his personal business any more than his twin did. Poor guy. He'd been dealing with two sisters for months now, but how long would it take to get used to the double-barreled powerhouse pair they'd become?

Leaning against the kitchen countertop, Gray accepted a cold glass of water from Maddie.

"You don't see me sweating it. No rush. God can take all the time He needs." What a lie. Sounded good, but didn't have much substance. He was ready to settle down. Start a family. But his profession of choice was proving to be a detriment. "Besides, there are enough weddings in the works for one family."

Not only was Jack engaged, but Maddie recently pledged herself to the Colby Ranch's foreman, Ty Garland. And Violet had caught the eye of one of Maddie's old beaus, Landon Derringer. A lot had happened during the months Grayson had been on his undercover assignment.

Jack held his gaze with a knowing one of his own, probably seeing through to the reality of Gray's marital protests, his allegiance to the bachelor way of life. A guy had his pride, after all.

"Always room for one more wedding, bro."

What his brother didn't mention, though, is that the siblings had come to the same conclusion. Until their dad returned safely—and Belle recovered—no one would be tying any knots. As much as Gray didn't like to think about it, how long would they stick with that vow if the weeks and months drew out? Belle had been in a coma since midsummer, with no sign of rejoining the world. Maddie and Landon had journeyed to south Texas in August to look for their dad. Keira and Jack tried again in September. Would their father turn up at Thanksgiving as he'd originally planned—or not?

While he couldn't do anything but pray for their mother, Gray could continue the search for his dad. He'd already filed a missing person's report and put his law-enforcement channels to good use.

But would his efforts be enough?

With so many issues about their parentage in turmoil and Belle so badly off, he needed to deliver to his family a positive outcome for their dad's situation. That would be one step in the right direction for a happily-ever-after on all counts.

And in spite of protests to the contrary, meeting a certain pretty brunette had him admitting he wouldn't mind settling down with a happily-ever-after of his own.

Chapter Three

"Hurry up, Cory." Elise glanced back at her lagging son as she walked briskly to their vehicle in the dimly lit grocery-store parking lot. Purse secured. Keys in hand. Her gaze alert to their surroundings.

Normally she shopped for groceries on Saturday morning, especially in the fall and winter as days grew shorter and didn't allow much time for after-work errands. Thank goodness for daylight savings time, but it would expire in another month. Unfortunately, she'd forgotten until this evening that she'd promised to make a red velvet cake for their youth pastor's birthday potluck after church tomorrow. She couldn't find a single drop of red food coloring in the kitchen cabinets.

"Mom?" Cory crawled into his seat and she locked the doors. Started the car.

"What?"

"When's Officer Wallace coming to the school again?"

As the overhead interior light faded, she looked into her son's hopeful eyes. He'd talked nonstop about Officer Wallace for the past twenty-four hours. How cool his badge was. How he'd brought him the ball glove. How he knew Daddy was a hero and said it was an honor to meet his son.

She offered a sympathetic smile. "Career day is once a year. It's doubtful he'll be back anytime soon."

The glow in his eyes faded momentarily, then brightened. "Maybe he'll come to visit anyway, to say hi to the kids."

She didn't want Cory to get his hopes up. The likelihood of Officer Wallace's return was slim. Yes, he'd made a memorable impression on them both, but it didn't take long for reality to set in. For her guard to go up. It was best for all concerned that Officer Wallace keep his distance. Unless she called the number on his business card, she suspected he would.

But she wouldn't call him. Not even for Cory. Especially not for Cory. Another cop in his life was too risky.

She smiled again at her son as she put the vehicle in gear and backed it out of the parking place. "He has an important job, sweetheart, so it's doubtful he could stop by even if he'd like to."

"I wish he would."

Heading into the darkened street, anxious to get home, she almost caught her own wishes echoing her son's.

But that was stupid.

And she wasn't a stupid woman.

Gazing down at the comatose Belle Colby, hooked up to medical paraphernalia of every imaginable kind, Grayson harbored the same frustration as his siblings at not being able to get desperately needed answers to their questions.

Although his siblings had picked up rumors from a former neighbor of the then still-intact family, what was the *real* reason Belle and his dad split? Why had they separated Maddie and him from their twin counterparts? The boys had been two, the girls not much beyond six months. Why had his father led him to believe Sharla Wallace was his birth mom?

Grayson gripped the black, leather-bound Bible in his hands. Did Belle know who'd sent these Bibles to him, his twin brother and two sisters? He and Maddie had received

them in June, after their dad headed out on his six-month
medical mission and not long before Grayson went undercover. No postmark. No return address. Later, Violet had
found one on the seat of her car after church and Jack's had
turned up on the hearth of the home he was renovating.

They all held the same handwritten, anonymous note, the
words of which were burned into his memory.

*I am sorry for what I did to you and your family. I hope
you and your siblings, especially your twin, can forgive me
as I ask the Lord to forgive me.*

When he and Maddie each received a Bible and identical note, they'd initially been puzzled. Then they'd laughed
them off, thinking someone had them confused with somebody else. At that point they hadn't any idea they each had
a twin. But *someone* had known—and for some reason felt
guilty about it.

Who? And why?

Gray shook his head as he continued to watch the quiet
rise and fall of Belle's breathing. Would she ever be able to
answer their questions?

The most pressing question of all, however, was where was
his dad? No one thought much about it when he didn't return
calls while on a mission trip. He wasn't big on checking in
and worked in remote areas with limited phone reception.
Then in August it was discovered he'd left his cell phone at
one of his stops in Blackstone, Texas. Probably got hundreds
of miles down the road before he realized it, intending to
swing back and get it later. Not too much concern at that time.

But in September when Grayson returned from his assignment, the family enlisted him to find their dad so they
could get answers to their family mystery. Not long into his
search he'd learned that his father appeared unwell at one
location. Jack had followed up, going down to search the
migrant camp where he'd last been spotted. He'd come up
empty-handed except to confirm that when last seen, their

father appeared feverish, coughing and maybe not quite lucid at times. Now they were greatly concerned and Gray's own investigation had escalated.

His heart heavy, he sat down in a molded plastic chair next to the bed, placing the mystery Bible on his knee. From the moment he laid eyes on her, he'd had no doubt that Belle was his mother. All the kids including him looked like her. None of them resembled their father. Although he hadn't yet looked into her eyes, he'd seen almost three decades' worth of photographs of her when he'd first come to the home of his long-lost siblings.

For the thousandth time in the past four weeks, he willed himself to remember something—anything—of his first two years with his birth mom. But not even a shadow of her remained.

Incredibly, the woman he and Maddie adored and had grown up believing was their mother *wasn't* their birth mother, although she *was* their little brother, Carter's, mom. The whole thing seemed like a dream—or a nightmare. He still hadn't grasped that Violet and Jack had lived separate lives, raised by this woman whose life he and Maddie should have shared as well.

He reached for his mother's warm but seemingly lifeless hand. Ran his thumb over the back of it. Said a silent prayer, then spoke aloud. "It's me, Grayson. Jack's brother. Your son."

Did that sound weird or what?

She didn't stir.

"I, uh, understand you never wanted Jack and Violet to pursue finding their father." He cleared his throat. "But we need to track Dad down. Let him know what's going on here. I know he's okay. He's gotten caught up in his work like he often does. He's a doctor now. A good one. Did you know that? A missionary doctor much of the time."

He shook his head, wondering about the wisdom of pouring all this out to the woman in the bed. Could she even hear him? Understand any of it?

"I'm a police officer in Fort Worth. That's why the others are counting on me to find him. I'm sorry if that's not what you want us to do. We don't mean for it to upset you."

He gently squeezed her motionless hand. "But don't you worry. Things will turn out fine. All of us kids are grateful we've found each other. Maddie's even moved from Fort Worth and will be marrying your ranch foreman, Ty. Doesn't that beat all?"

He paused to catch his breath, not used to rambling on in a soliloquy. "Violet and Jack are both engaged to fine folks, too. Keira's a vet, which will come in handy at the ranch, and Landon's an old friend of mine. So lots of weddings in the works, and we need you there to help out."

Silence permeated the room, except for the wall clock ticking away the seconds as he breathed in the antiseptic scents clinging to the Spartan space.

"Nothing in the plans like that for me." He chuckled, but memory flashed unbidden to the captivating Elise Lopez. Why couldn't he get her out of his head? "So don't go getting your hopes up. I think I'm destined to go it alone. You know, the dedicated lawman route."

"Oh, yeah, the dedicated lawman," a familiar female voice whispered from the doorway. His sister. The original one. Maddie. "Leaving scores of women pining in his wake."

With a grin, he turned to look at her. Who'd have thought a polished, twenty-five-year-old former assistant at the glamorous *Texas Today* magazine would be standing here in Western-flavored garb, hair swept into a ponytail? She still had a stylish city flair, but what a difference a few months had made.

"Pining women, huh?" He stood, tucked the Bible under his slinged arm and quietly moved to join her in the hallway. "You know something I don't know?"

"Hey, I have more than a few girlfriends at *Texas Today* who still talk about the time you escorted me to that company cookout. Believe me, they'd sell their BMWs for a chance to get their hands on you."

"Would hate for them to make that kind of sacrifice for a sorry specimen like me."

"Yeah, right." Maddie grinned, then motioned to the doorway behind him. "So how's…Belle today? Seems strange to call her Mom, doesn't it?"

"Can't do it myself."

Maddie rested a hand on his arm and they moved a short distance down the hall, out of Belle's earshot—if she could hear them at all.

"But she is our mother, Gray. You and Jack might have doubts about your male parentage, but you only have to take one look at her and know we're hers."

His spine stiffened. "I don't have any doubts about my male parentage. I'm not buying into that Fort Worth woman's tales. She sounds like a troublemaker to me. Dad's my dad and that's all there is to it."

No way would he even speculate he was Joe Earl's offspring—a guy that on the best of days you wouldn't brag about being related to. He didn't care that his siblings had talked to a neighbor where their parents originally lived in Fort Worth. Patty Earl, the deceased Joe Earl's wife, seemed to know all about them. Even claimed her man had gotten a sixteen-year-old Belle pregnant with twin boys twenty-eight years ago. She said Belle had tricked Brian into marrying her, claiming they were his and all but implying that's why Belle and Brian divorced shortly after the birth of a second set of twins.

He wasn't buying it. Brian Wallace was his father. Period. He believed that. He *had* to believe it. It's all he had to hang on to now. The one thing that kept the fragile balance of his world upright in the midst of the onslaught of family revelations.

His brother wasn't quite as sure. He'd never had a father in his life. Didn't understand why his abandoned him. It probably made more sense that if Brian Wallace wasn't his biological father, that could account for his being willing to walk away from him, to let part of the family go.

Maddie's brow crinkled. "So you don't think—?"

"No."

She studied him with concern and he realized his expression was likely as fierce as his thoughts.

"I didn't mean to upset you, Gray."

"You didn't. I've got a lot on my mind after what we all talked about at breakfast." His siblings' hopes of finding their dad—who held the answers their mother was incapable of providing—focused more and more on him.

"His being out of touch isn't unheard of." Maddie accurately tracked his thoughts. "But why'd Dad have to do a disappearing act in the middle of this family mess? From what you and Jack found out, he may be terribly ill. We've got to find him. You know, before…"

His jaw tightened as her words drifted off, but he knew where she'd been headed. They needed to find him—alive and well.

"I'm doing my best."

She lifted her chin as if challenging her fears and gave him a resolute smile. "Then he's as good as found."

He wished he could reassure his sister. Tell her there was nothing to worry about. But the situation wasn't promising at this point. He'd like to think people didn't disappear into thin air, but from his cop standpoint he knew it happened. He didn't want his dad becoming one of those disheartening statistics.

Maddie gazed at him thoughtfully, her voice low. "Between the two of us, how are you feeling about the rest of this? The twin thing, I mean. Finding out that Mom isn't our birth mom. I know you dragged your feet, found every excuse under the sun not to see…Belle. Or face your brother."

He scoffed. "Excuses? That's what you call my job and physical therapy? My trying to find Dad?"

"You could have found a way to get here sooner than last weekend and we both know it. But I didn't push you because I remember how it felt the first time I encountered Violet."

So he hadn't concealed his mixed-up feelings about the situation as well as he thought he had. He'd essentially talked himself into thinking he could only adequately conduct an investigation into his father's status from Fort Worth. That he didn't need to beat a path to Grasslands the moment he'd heard from Maddie. Had he thought if he delayed coming out here it might all go away? That he'd wake up one morning and none of this would have happened? It would again be just him, Maddie and Carter. Their dad and the memories of their mother.

His sister squeezed his arm. "At breakfast this morning, you still seemed a little freaked out with Jack sitting across from you wearing your face."

Gray scowled. "Wearing *my* face? Not hardly. I see a family resemblance, sure, like we're brothers. Or cousins. But I don't get everyone thinking we're matching bookends."

Maddie yelped a laugh as he'd hoped she would. Get her mind off the seriousness of their family situation.

"Look at you," a gravelly male voice intruded. "Finally got yourself a haircut, did you, boy? About time."

Puzzled, Gray turned toward a stout, forty-something man sauntering down the tiled floor toward them. Dressed in jeans and a tan uniform shirt, a Western felt hat in hand, a smile spread across the balding man's face. He stopped beside Gray, giving him a thorough inspection.

"Have to admit you clean up good." He chuckled, smacking the side of his leg with the hat. "But I never figured you to be one to let that fiancée of yours dress you up like a Ken doll."

"Pardon?" Gray glanced at Maddie, whose eyes danced with mischief.

"George, this isn't Jack Colby. This is his twin brother, Grayson Wallace. He's visiting from Fort Worth."

The man drew back, squinting to give Gray a more thorough scrutiny—from the collar of his navy knit polo shirt, past neatly pressed gray trousers and down to the tips of polished leather shoes.

"I'll be swallowed by a horned toad. Shoulda known Jack wouldn't let a pretty little lady pry those Tony Lamas offa his feet." Shaking his head with a lopsided smile, he thrust out a hand to grasp Grayson's. "Good to meet you, son. Heard about the goings-on at the Colby Ranch. Two sets of twins who didn't know the others were alive. Don't that beat all."

"Mighty wild," Gray acknowledged, amazed at how well-informed a small-town grapevine could be. Must be a piece of cake being a lawman around here. No need for undercover assignments—you camped out at the local diner and kept your ears open.

"Gray," Maddie chimed in as she looked from one man to the other, "this is George Cole, our sheriff. George, Grayson's a police officer in Fort Worth. He's building a respectable reputation for himself back there and his superiors have their eye on him for a move up in the ranks."

He never should have confided in her. Put like that, it sounded like bragging, even if he wasn't the one doing it.

"You don't say." George squinted again, as if sizing up Gray anew. "Don't suppose, then, that you'll be movin' out this way with the rest of your kin like your sister here did?"

"No plans to, sir."

"Think about it, young'un. Serious like. Opportunity is knockin' at your door. We've got ourselves a deputy retiring come the end of the year. Lookin' for a replacement."

Grayson managed not to laugh. What did they do all day in this sleepy Texas Mayberry? Play checkers and arrest people for overdue library fines? No, he couldn't see himself as a Barney Fife to this guy's Andy Taylor.

"Thank you kindly, but home's Fort Worth."

George chortled as he turned his hat in his hands. "Don't let the laid-back trappings of our little cow-town community scare you off, boy. If you've a mind to join the family hereabouts, we'd fit you right in. Could get that city-slicker veneer washed offa you before you can say 'Alamo.' What do you think, Maddie?"

She turned appraising eyes on her older brother. "I'd love for Gray to move out here. He'd look mighty handsome in boots and a Stetson."

"See, son? Family ties trump city life and a hotshot career any day."

"It's tempting, but I have commitments elsewhere."

George squinted and gave him a knowing nod. "Shoulda figured as much. Strapping young man like you must have a special lady."

Gray's memory flashed to Elise Lopez and at once Maddie slipped to his side and hooked her arm through his, her eyes narrowing.

"A special lady, is it, big bro?" Her tone echoed with mock accusation. "I think we need to have ourselves a private chat."

"Sorry for blowing the whistle on you and running, son." The sheriff's eyes twinkled as he set his hat on his shiny pate and turned away. "But I have to make my rounds. Stopped in to check on my granny. She broke her leg chasing a calf out of the kitchen yesterday."

Calf? Or had the man said *cat?* Baffled, Gray fixed his gaze on the lawman striding away, but he sensed Maddie's eyes boring into him.

"So, Gray, let's hear it. All of it."

He turned to her. "All of what?"

"About that special lady."

He adjusted the sling and secured the Bible under his arm. He didn't want to explain Elise Lopez. What could he say? That she was one of the most intriguing women he'd met in a good long while—and she wouldn't give him the time of day? "Sorry to disappoint you, Mad, but there's been no lady in my life since Jenna showed me the door. The commitment I was referring to is my career."

"When George made that little lady assumption, you got one of those deer-in-the-headlights looks in your eyes. The kind you had as a kid when you were hiding something and Dad called your bluff."

"Contrary to your belief, the world has more than its fair share of women who aren't keen on getting involved with a cop."

"Jenna didn't have the sense of a goose."

Or maybe she was one wise woman?

Regardless, he suspected Elise Lopez had plenty of common sense on her side—and she clearly wanted nothing to do with him. Despite the fact that for some inexplicable reason he'd left his business card with her, he wasn't accustomed to pursuing women who didn't show obvious interest.

Maybe it was his pride, but he didn't intend to start now.

Chapter Four

"**M**om!" Cory yelled from the living room Sunday evening. "It's Officer Wallace. And look what he brought me."

Cory's cop was back?

A knot twisted in Elise's stomach as she hurried from the bedroom, wishing she had time to slip bare feet into shoes and change out of her sweat suit. As she approached the door open to the hallway, Cory's grin widened under the brim of a Western straw hat—and beyond him she glimpsed Grayson Wallace standing respectfully off to one side, head bowed as if analyzing the worn carpet.

"Isn't this awesome? Wait until I show Kyle. Can I, Mom?"

"It's a school night."

"I know, but please?" His eyes begged. "I'll hurry."

While it wasn't long before bedtime, Kyle was Billie Jean's seventh-grader in the apartment below—and she'd rather not talk to Officer Wallace in Cory's presence. Apparently the lawman hadn't gotten the message that only her son welcomed police officers with open arms. "Okay. But I expect you back here in ten minutes."

"Yee haw!" Cory dashed out the door, high-fiving the cop as he went by. "This is way cool. I can be a sheriff. Or a Texas Ranger."

Turning toward Cory's cop, she caught his look of dismay. Had he actually believed the hat would distract her son from all things police related?

She stepped into the hallway, pulling the door partially closed behind her. She'd planned to straighten the apartment once Cory had gone to sleep, but Mr. Wallace didn't need a glimpse of her chaotic, real-life world. "Nice try with the hat, but you didn't need to do that."

He smiled uncertainly, as if not sure of the reception his unannounced call would elicit. "I know I didn't. But I figured it might get his mind off cops and onto cowboys. From the sound of that departing comment, though, I struck out."

Was that the true reason he'd stopped by? Or did he have something else on his mind? "I'm not sure aspiring to a career in rodeo would be much safer than law enforcement."

"But what are the chances he'll make it to bull and bronc riding?" His eyes twinkled. "A lot of the pros started out on goats and calves before they were out of diapers. I don't see a whole lot of opportunity for that around here."

"True. But I'm sorry after all your effort he's not cooperating. Thanks for going out of your way to try."

"Easy enough to do. I was in the western part of the state over the weekend—I have family out that way—and saw the hat in a truck stop. I thought to myself, 'Self, you know a boy who would look mighty fine in a hat like that.'"

His grin urged her heart into a full gallop.

"Western Texas? You're not from Fort Worth?"

"Actually I am, but I recently discovered a branch of the family I previously didn't know existed. Cattle ranchers."

She couldn't help but smile. "So you're taking up riding and roping and making yourself at home with shirttail kin?"

He tilted his head and squinted one eye. "A tad closer than shirttail. A twin brother and a second little sister."

She stared. "You have a *twin* that you didn't know about?"

"Long story." He grimaced as if wishing he hadn't mentioned it, then a purposeful gleam sparked in his eyes. "But I didn't stop by to regale you with the particulars of my family tree or just to drop off the hat."

Uh-oh. Here it comes.

Why couldn't men leave her in peace? She wasn't in the market for another man. And certainly not this one. Yes, even with the sturdy sling supporting his arm, he looked like any woman's dream standing there fit and trim in pressed khaki trousers, his wide shoulders filling out a burgundy golf shirt. But she was all too aware how innocent dreams revolving around a cop could morph into nightmares.

"Mr. Wallace—"

"Grayson." Determination etched his features. "On Friday Cory's teacher asked if I'd consider talking to you about mentoring Cory. I've considered it, and I'm here to discuss it."

He was, was he? She folded her arms. Out of the blue this stranger wanted to spend time with her son? Become his role model? Was he out of his mind? *Does he think I'm out of mine?* Since Duke's passing, she'd had men come up with doozies of excuses to worm their way into her life, but this got top honors for originality.

"You know," the officer prodded when she didn't immediately respond, "I could give him some man time."

With a cop? What was Cory's teacher thinking? That could exacerbate her son's fixation.

"I'm sorry, but—"

He raised a hand to halt her. "I didn't say anything on Friday, but since then I've had time to think about it. So if you feel it would be beneficial in any way, if it might help Cory settle down and—"

"*Settle down?* Exactly what did Miss Gilbert tell you about my son?" She'd have a talk with her tomorrow.

His forehead creased. "Don't get riled up at Cory's teacher. She said pretty much what you told me yourself. You know, that he's preoccupied with policemen. She thinks he's overly concerned about the man who killed his father and is aggressively acting out on his feelings."

"That term is considerably stronger than the situation warrants."

"Likely so. Nevertheless, Miss Gilbert is worried about him and noticed how Cory and I hit it off that day."

"She means well, but doesn't fully understand the situation." Did Miss Gilbert think so little of her parenting abilities that she felt a need to push Cory off on a man she didn't even know? The implication stung. Elise forced a smile. "Thank you for stopping by, but teaming my son with a police officer—after the loss of his father in the line of duty—isn't a good idea."

"I understand, but—"

"I appreciate your considerate offer, but it's not in Cory's best interests."

From out of nowhere, her son galloped down the hallway to slip by her and into the apartment. She stepped back inside, as well.

"Have a good evening, Officer Wallace."

With a quick glance in his direction, she closed the door.

Monday after work as Gray grilled supper on the enclosed patio outside his ground-floor condo, the rejection of the night before still stung.

The sole consolation was how pretty Elise had looked in her velour sweats as she delivered the dismissal, dainty pink-painted toenails peeping below the soft, shapely pants. Her hair, loose from its customary bun, cascaded down her back. She smelled good, too. Like roses in his mom's garden back in Appleton.

He turned the steak over, its juices sizzling in the low flame as he savored the memory of Ms. Lopez attired for a relaxing Sunday evening at home, bare feet and all. Was it his fault he could almost envision her cuddled up beside him on the sofa, soft and warm, watching Sunday Night Football?

He had to admit, though, that while her curt dismissal of his suggestion to spend time with Cory rankled, he was genuinely relieved. He'd volunteered because he felt obligated, not due to a driving need to get involved with some woman's kid again.

If this past weekend his sister Violet hadn't told him of the challenges she and Jack faced growing up without a dad, he'd have minded his own business. If Maddie hadn't shared the struggles her soon-to-be stepdaughter experienced when her father had been absent during her earliest years, or Gray hadn't been reminded of the impact the church youth coach Reggie Lenard had on his own life, he'd never have considered it.

If he hadn't seen that stupid cowboy hat in a truck stop…

So, bottom line, he was good with being let off the hook. God was looking out for him, as He had the night he'd dived off that balcony to elude an unhappy guy with a gun.

His plate was already stacked high enough, what with physical therapy to get a dislocated shoulder back in shape and trying to find his dad. He'd scheduled a few days off this week to devote time to the latter pursuit. He could only hope and pray he'd be the bearer of good news soon.

He'd pulled the steak from the grill and deposited it onto a plate when his cell phone rang. He didn't recognize the number as work or family related, but maybe it was someone responding to a query about his dad's whereabouts.

"Wallace."

"Grayson Wallace?"

The lilting, feminine tone didn't sound like your typical telemarketer.

"Speaking."

"This is Elise Lopez—Cory's mother."

Well, well, well. He eased himself into a nearby patio

chair, picturing her as he'd last seen her—arms folded and dark eyes pleading with him to get lost. Sensing the armor around her from the moment their gazes first met at the school, he had no idea how he'd gotten up the nerve to hand her his business card. She'd probably thought it a mighty bold move. After last night's send-off, he never expected she'd use it. Had she thought of yet another reason why having him around wouldn't be in her son's best interests and was dying to share it with him?

"I'm sorry to disturb you this evening," she rushed breathlessly as if wanting to get the call over with as quickly as possible, "but I'm afraid I've underestimated the situation with Cory's adjustment to school. Do you have time to meet with me this evening? If it's not too inconvenient, at the coffee shop across the street from the clinic where I work?"

He gave a longing glance at his cooling dinner, but sat up straighter at the note of urgency in her voice. "I can do that."

"Thank you."

"Is everything…okay?" Dumb question. Of course it wasn't or she wouldn't be talking to him at the moment. It didn't take a genius to figure out calling a cop for a favor— any cop—was clearly an act of desperation.

"It looks as if—" her words came softly in his ear "—I'll be taking you up on your offer to spend time with Cory."

"I got a call from the school early this afternoon." Elise leaned forward in the coffee-shop booth next to a window, arms resting on the table as she took in the concerned countenance of the last man on earth she wanted to turn to for help. "He's been suspended for two days. For fighting. And not just fighting, but for starting the fights."

Grayson frowned. "Fights. As in plural."

"Yes." Could he hear the shame in her words? Know how hard she fought to keep her lips from trembling?

"The first time when playing cops and robbers during recess and he didn't get picked to be a cop. A relatively minor scuffle. But later in the day there was an altercation in the lunchroom. Cory was showing a classmate a picture of his dad in uniform and an older boy made a comment about Duke not being too bright if he stood there and let someone shoot him." She took a steadying breath. "I guess that was all it took. Cory bloodied his nose. Another kid joined in and the next thing you know—"

"You've got a brawl."

"Yes."

"Was Cory hurt?"

Her lips tightened. "Minor scrapes. Bruises. The other boys the same. Nothing of a serious nature…but enough to get him suspended."

"Were the other boys suspended, too?" To her relief, he sounded as if he was in Cory's corner, making sure he hadn't been singled out for punishment.

"One day. Cory got two because both times he threw the first punch."

Gray let out a gust of breath. "He must have been pushed to the max. My gut instinct is that Cory isn't a violent-natured kid."

So did that mean he was willing to help Cory?

She toyed with the coffee mug in front of her. She hadn't taken a single sip. Grayson's mug, likewise, sat neglected.

"I spent the afternoon in the school counselor's office."

"Does Cory understand the ramifications of what he did? That you had to miss work?"

"I explained that I have to take those hours off without pay or use vacation time that I could have otherwise spent doing something fun with him."

"And he apologized?"

"To me? Yes. And to his principal and the lunchroom monitor." She leaned back in the booth seat, recalling the humiliation of the meeting in the counselor's office. "A couple of the other boys have been in trouble before. Their parents shrugged the whole thing off when I made him apologize to them. It was almost as if they were proud their kids held their own in a fight that warranted a suspension. But I'm ashamed."

"You weren't the one who landed a punch."

"No, but I should have been more alert to how deeply the loss of his father has impacted him. It's been several months since he's cried about anything, no matter how upset. Even today, not a single tear. He'd seemed to be adjusting. Did well in kindergarten, but now..."

"Sounds like the other boys know what buttons to push."

She solemnly traced a finger along the rim of the coffee mug. "Unfortunately."

"So what do you have in mind? For Cory and me, I mean."

A young, dark-haired waitress paused at their table and the conversation momentarily halted. The teenager appeared surprised that neither had touched their aromatic brew, but discreetly departed without comment.

Elise pushed her coffee aside. "Miss Gilbert and Mrs. Clifton, his counselor, suggested I take you up on your offer to spend time with him. To see if a responsible male can instill positive reinforcement before—" she paused, then forced the words "—before we seek professional help. I don't have the financial means for a psychologist, and my insurance doesn't cover that type of thing. Of course, I'll do whatever it takes to help Cory, take out a loan if necessary, but—"

"Elise." Grayson rested a palm on the table, his expression earnest. "When Miss Gilbert approached me about entering the mentoring program, I was dead set against it. I'm not a trained counselor. I'm not even involved in the youth programs at church. I'm not qualified to handle a situation like this."

"But you offered." Why did she have to sound so desperate? So needy? What was she doing here begging this man for assistance?'

"I know I did, but—"

"But that was before he turned—" she almost choked on the word "—violent."

The flattened hand on the table fisted. "Decking a kid who was asking for it is unfortunate. There's a definite anger control issue coming into play. But Cory isn't, in my estimation, turning violent."

She let out a soft sigh of relief. "When you made the offer last night, you must have thought you could help."

Gray grimaced. "It's a long story which I won't go into, but I know of a situation… I learned over the weekend how growing up without a father can affect someone."

The recently discovered brother and sister he'd mentioned earlier?

"So you see," he continued, "I'd come back home with my Superman cape on, thinking I could make a difference for Cory by bringing him the hat and hanging out with him. But I'm not educationally qualified for something like this."

"You need a degree to hang out with a six-year-old? Play games? Help with homework? Just talk?"

"No, but—"

She leaned forward, swallowing her pride as she appealed on her son's behalf. "He admires you. Looks up to you. Maybe he'll open up and tell you why he's angry with the world."

Grayson tapped a finger on the table, his frank gaze meeting hers. "I can already tell you why he's angry with the world."

He knew? It was so simple and she'd missed it?

"Why?"

"Because the world he trusted betrayed him. Turned itself upside down. Took his dad away from him and probably took you away from him in a number of ways as well."

There had to be more to it than that. A reason why his anger was coming out now instead of in kindergarten. She quietly studied him, then took a stab in the dark. "For someone who isn't degreed in kid psych, you seem sure of your assessment. Personal experience?"

He glanced away to stare out the window, beyond his own reflection, at the passing traffic headlights penetrating the last dregs of twilight. "I didn't lose my father, but my mom died in a car accident when I was seven."

"I'm sorry." She shouldn't have probed into his painful past. "That had to have been difficult."

"It was a long time ago."

"But you still remember." She sensed it. Suspected it might play a role in his final decision on Cory's behalf. "You weren't much older than Cory. Maybe you can make him understand what's going on down deep inside."

"Maybe. But it sounds as if he needs someone to step in immediately, before things escalate." He paused, his expression grave. "I don't know what it entails for training and all, but it could easily take a month or more for me to get approved for the school's mentoring program."

"Then we don't go through the mentoring program."

Something she couldn't decipher flickered through his eyes.

His words came carefully. "It's a standard—and wise— practice to conduct a background check. Which could take—"

"I did my own background check." She met his intent gaze with a challenging one of her own. "I contacted an old buddy of my husband's who contacted someone in your division. You passed with flying colors."

A brow quirked. "You didn't waste any time."

Did he approve? Disapprove? It didn't matter. She'd done what she had to do. "I've already wasted too much time because I didn't see this coming. Cory is too important to me to wait for weeks to go through official school district channels."

"I'm still not—"

"Please? A few nights a week? Even a single hour this weekend?"

"I'll be out of town this weekend." He must have seen the disappointment in her eyes, for he cleared his throat and continued. "But I'm taking a few days off. Tomorrow and Wednesday."

"I can't impose on your vacation."

"Personal business, not a true vacation. But I might have time available later in the afternoon."

She could tell by the still-uncertain look that he had lingering concerns, but she pressed for a firm commitment. "So you *will* spend time with him? See if he'll open up to you?"

He settled back in the booth, his eyes locked on hers. "I'll give it a shot. Tomorrow? Three-thirty?"

Impulsively she reached across the table to grasp his hand, an unexpected bolt of awareness darting through her as skin touched skin. "Thank you."

He gazed at their clasped hands a long moment, then back at her. "You'll tell Cory I'm coming?"

She hesitated. It might not be a good idea to get her son's hopes up. What if it didn't work out for him to come after all?

Grayson shifted, turning his hand in hers to give it a reassuring squeeze. "You can tell him, Elise. I promise I won't be a no-show."

Relieved, she self-consciously withdrew her hand. Took a calming breath. "I've arranged for him to stay all day with his after-school sitter, Billie Jean. She lives in a ground-floor apartment directly below mine. I'll let her know you're coming."

"Don't expect any miracles, okay?" Grayson frowned as he massaged his injured shoulder. "We'll hang out. Get to know each other. But you've got to be prepared that he could change his mind about me. May not want anything to do with me. Or it could backfire entirely—ramp up his anger or what you call his cop obsession."

"That's a risk I have to take, isn't it?" She reluctantly drew her eyes from his too-magnetic gaze and stood, noting uneasily that the sky had fully darkened. "I have to go. I left Cory with Billie Jean. But I can't thank you enough, Mr. Wallace…Grayson."

She quickly turned away, hurried out the door and onto the street. Filling her lungs with the still-warm night air, she offered a silent word of thanks.

God was answering her tear-filled prayers.

But what was she getting Cory and herself into, allowing another police officer into their lives?

Chapter Five

What did he know about what went on in a little kid's head?

Gray stared at himself in the bathroom mirror Tuesday morning as he readied himself for the day. *Wallace, you may be known for having a cool, clear head on the job, but you're not even thinking straight.*

He'd agreed to spend one-on-one time with Cory. But how much of his decision was based on the hopeful glow in Elise's eyes last night at the coffee shop? The grateful sincerity in her voice touched a chord deep within. Had he agreed to help because he thought he could make a difference for Cory—or because it would be an excuse to spend time with the boy's mother?

He had to come up with something he could do with the kid. He couldn't sit across the table and interrogate him to get to the heart of his anger issues. Trying to force a confession for an easily resolved happily-ever-after would be bound to fail.

With his bum shoulder he couldn't even play catch like he used to do with Jenna's boy. What do you say to a kid whose dad died? And violently at that. People meant well enough when his own mom was killed on that long-ago, stormy night, but "your mother is in heaven" hadn't done a whole lot for him. It only served to upset his dad when his oldest child wakened in the night crying and begging God to return her.

After that, he didn't cry. Not in front of his father. Not in front of anyone. Is that why Cory didn't cry? He didn't want to upset his mother? Maybe he kept it all bottled up inside and when the opportunity came to unleash it in physical form—like knocking some smart aleck's block off—it wasn't worth the effort to try to restrain himself.

With a shake of his head, Gray reached for the razor. He had all morning and into the afternoon to decide what to do with Cory. Today he had to make headway on the search for his father, so he couldn't devote a lot of time obsessing about the boy's situation. Maybe God would have mercy on him and the kid would flatly tell his pretty mom he didn't want to see Officer Wallace today. Or ever.

Elise eased up on the gas pedal. She'd been keyed up all day wondering how things would go between Grayson and Cory during their hour together. What they would do. What they would talk about. Was this a wrong choice on her part? Would it appear to Cory he was being rewarded for yesterday's misbehavior?

At twenty till six, she rounded the final corner and pulled up in front of the apartment house behind a now-familiar silver SUV. *Grayson was still here?* Yes. Sitting on the concrete porch talking to a rapt Cory.

She'd no more than stepped out of her vehicle when a diminutive Volkswagen pulled in behind her, the logo of a popular pizzeria adorning its roof. A teenage boy dashed by her, carrying a paper bag and large flat box. Grayson rose to pull out his wallet as Cory welcomed the pizza with open arms. By the teen's euphoric smile, she imagined the tip made the delivery worthwhile.

As the pizza guy jogged back to his car, she approached the twosome again seated on the concrete porch steps, checking out the contents of the box. Cory looked up, grin widening.

"Mom! Officer Wallace bought us pizza! My favorite, pepperoni. And part ham and pineapple, *your* favorite!"

"What's the occasion of this celebratory feast?" She turned an inquiring eye on Grayson who was casually dressed in jeans, tennis shoes and a gray zippered sweatshirt, looking even more handsome than he had last night. She hoped the pizza didn't mean she had to invite him in, though. She hadn't cleaned up the breakfast dishes before dashing off to work this morning. The bathroom and kitchen were in need of a deep cleaning, too. Why couldn't she keep up with the simplest of chores?

"Cory said he hadn't had pizza in a while and I realized I hadn't either, so we decided to give the cook a break tonight."

She glanced at her son, hoping the reality wasn't that he'd begged his new friend for takeout. Mother and son might have a generic frozen pizza when on sale, but rarely a fresh, popular pizzeria variety. So this was a treat for both of them. "Thank you. What a nice welcome home."

"Mom! Guess what?" Cory pulled paper plates and a wad of napkins from the bag and handed them to Grayson, then snagged himself a slice of pizza. "He's teaching me what the police codes are on the radio scanner."

She forced a smile. Grayson had warned her his presence might ramp up Cory's fascination with policemen, but did he have to feed the overactive interest with cop talk?

Cory took a bite out of his pepperoni slice. No point in embarrassing him in front of his new friend, but she'd remind him later about waiting for others to be served—and washing his hands. He chewed rapidly, then swallowed before fishing a small white card out of his back pocket and waving it at her.

"Look, Mom. He gave me his business card. It has his cell

number on it and everything. He even wrote his address so I can send him a letter."

"How nice." Despite her dismay, she managed a smile in Grayson's direction. "Looks like you've made a friend."

His questioning gaze held hers for a lingering moment, as if trying to gauge her underlying reaction to Cory's enthusiasm. "It's a nice night. Cooled off some. We thought we'd sit out here picnic-style if that's okay with you."

It was more than okay with her. "May I get you something to drink, Grayson? Soda? Tea? Water?" At least she thought there were still a few sodas in the refrigerator. She didn't buy them often.

"Soda!" Cory, who'd stuffed another bite of pizza into his mouth, nevertheless managed to yell through the wad of dough and tomato sauce.

She shot him a mind-your-manners look. "Milk for you."

"Aw, Mom." Cory stomped his foot and reached for another slice of pizza.

Grayson gave her a sympathetic smile. "Water for me."

"Me, too. Two waters and a milk, coming right up." She excused herself and, once inside the apartment, she dashed to the bedroom to peel out of her work clothes before slipping into a pair of faded jeans and a fine-gauge sweater suitable for the mild evening.

She paused in front of the mirror. Ugh. She looked like a stereotypical worn-out schoolmarm with her hair up in a bun like that. It served its purpose at the clinic, keeping it out of her way and lending her a no-nonsense professional edge with incoming clients. But she looked so stuffy.

With only a second's hesitation, she released her hair from its confines. Shook it loose. Bent over and ran her fingers through it, then straightened for another look at her reflection. No, that was *too* much.

She quickly braided it down her back, a happy compromise. Or was it? Why did she care if Grayson Wallace thought she looked like the prim school teacher on *Little House on the Prairie* reruns? With a frown, she coiled the braid at the back of her head and secured it with hairclips, then prepared their drinks in plastic tumblers and headed downstairs.

"So what else did you do today?" She distributed the drinks and seated herself on the far side of Cory. Grayson held out the open pizza box so she could slide two slices onto a paper plate. She murmured her thanks, deliberately avoiding his gaze.

"We kicked the soccer ball around. And Officer Wallace showed me dribbling tricks. Is that cool or what?"

"Very cool." She took a bite of pizza, relishing the blend of sharp Italian spices mingling with the sweet pineapple and smoky-flavored ham, then wiped her lips with a napkin. When had she ever been so self-conscious eating pizza?

Cory appeared on top of the world, but she didn't know Grayson well enough to read his personal take on the day. He had on that all-too-familiar expressionless look she used to call Duke's "cop face." Carefully guarded. Giving nothing away.

"Is it okay if Officer Wallace comes tomorrow, too, Mom?"

Would he be up for back-to-back kid duty? "I'm not sure he'll have time two days in a row, Cory."

Her son turned to Grayson. "Can you, sir? It would be awesome."

Grayson caught her eye, then smiled at Cory. "Why don't I talk it over with your mother first."

"Please, Mom! Let him come."

"We'll see."

For the next twenty minutes, Elise sat mostly in silence as she listened in on Cory and Grayson's conversation. Surprisingly, Grayson seemed up-to-date on kid flicks, video games and the latest toys that captured a boy's imagination. Perhaps he had a nephew? Or could there be a son of his own?

He had an easy way of talking with Cory, allowing the boy to speak and prompting him with questions that encouraged him to continue. Cory ate it up, basking in Grayson's attention. Ever so grateful, a heaviness nevertheless settled in the region of her heart. These were the shared moments that Duke should have been indulging his son in. Not a stranger.

As twilight settled in around them, she gently reminded Cory it was time to go inside and get started on the homework she'd picked up from the school on her lunch hour.

His brows lowered and for a moment she thought he would argue, but with a quick glance at Grayson he got to his feet. "Don't forget, Mom, you said this could be a skip night."

"I remember. I'll come up in a few minutes." She handed him her door key.

"Good night, Officer Wallace." Admiration oozed from her son's voice.

"Good night, Cory." Grayson stretched out a hand for a shake. "I enjoyed our time together today."

"Me, too. I hope tomorrow you can—" Cory shot a look at her, then clammed up.

He whirled to race in the door, feet clomping up the stairs. Cringing at the loud reverberation, Elise rose as well, hoping the other apartment dwellers didn't complain about the commotion.

Grayson stood, curiosity lighting his eyes. "Skip night?"

She self-consciously brushed imagined pizza crumbs from her sweater. "On Fridays—and other special nights—he doesn't have to take a bath."

His rumbling laugh warmed her. "All boy."

"Oh, yes." She smiled, too. "Judging from Cory's enthusiasm, you two must have continued to hit it off."

"We did."

There was no point in beating around the bush. She'd

asked Grayson to spend time with Cory for a purpose. "Did he talk about what happened yesterday?"

Grayson scuffed the toe of his shoe at a crack in the concrete sidewalk, as if weighing his words. "He told me about it. Part of it, at least."

"And?"

"If I was six years old, I'd have decked the kid, too."

She grimaced. "I hope you didn't tell him that."

"Trust me." His level gaze reinforced the words of assurance. "We talked about what makes us mad and why we can't punch people even if we don't agree with them. Not even when they hurt our feelings or tell a lie."

"Was he receptive to that?"

Grayson nodded. "He knows what he did was wrong. I can't guarantee you he won't do it again. Sometimes reflexes overcome brain cells. But I believe he's genuinely sorry, and not only because he got caught."

"That's the key, isn't it?"

"He's a good kid, Elise." He reached out as if intending to give her arm a reassuring pat, then thought better of it and lowered his arm to his side. "A few bumps in the road right now. But you're raising him right."

Her spirits rose at the approval shining in his eyes as he delivered the unsolicited compliment. Too often she doubted herself. Felt like the worst mother in the world. She offered a hopeful smile. "So you don't think my son's destined for juvenile detention?"

"Naw. He idolizes his dad. He's angry that bad people took him away from him." He paused and cocked his head to the side, his gaze assessing her. "And he worries about you."

"Me?"

"He says you work all the time or are studying. You're always saving money and won't buy yourself anything pretty."

What?

"That's not true. Why, I—" But when was the last time

she'd bought anything frivolous for herself? Not since Duke's death or, more accurately, not since she'd been approached by those to whom he owed money. Not since she sold Duke's truck and hunting rifles. The camping equipment, fishing boat. Furniture. The house. Not since all but the bare necessities had been carted off to consignment stores.

"Kids are observant," he noted softly, accurately reading her bewilderment. Then he paused to study the surrounding rundown homes. "So are you from around here?"

Judging from his question, it was clear he wondered how she'd come to live in a poorly maintained apartment in a so-so neighborhood when Duke's police-force wages and life insurance should have ensured a more comfortable lifestyle for his beneficiaries. He probably thought she'd run through Duke's money, a merry widow blowing the funds for which her husband had traded his life. Well, let him think whatever he wanted. It was none of his business.

"Actually, I'm from Arizona."

He leaned toward her. "Phoenix?"

"No, a small town. Canyon Springs. I'm sure you've never heard of it."

"Can't say I have. Believe it or not, I've never been to Arizona. Texas is hot enough for me—no interest in adding overgrown cactus to the mix."

Relieved at the change in topic, she smiled. "My hometown is in a beautiful mountain pine forest. Pleasantly cool in the summer and considerable snow in the winter. Not a saguaro in sight. But you Texans don't think any place compares to the Lone Star State, do you?"

"Not much needed that we can't find right here inside our own borders." Grayson chuckled at what he had to know was an arrogant-sounding admission. "So is that where your husband was from, too? This mountain country paradise?"

Back to Duke. But she'd keep her explanation brief.

"We were childhood sweethearts. He was several years

ahead of me in school and moved to Texas when he was twenty-one. Then I joined him when I graduated."

"You're giving me a hard time about Texas—" Grayson folded his arms, his tone teasing "—but you must like it here since you didn't head straight home to Arizona after—"

He cast her an apologetic glance as the allusion to her husband's death hung heavily between them.

"Texas grows on you." She forced a smile to break the awkwardness. "What's the old joke? I wasn't born here, but got here as fast as I could?"

A relieved grin touched his lips. Not only a strikingly handsome man, but a sensitive one as well.

"You said earlier," she rushed on, alarmed at the feelings his concern for her elicited, "that you're originally from Fort Worth?"

"Born here. Then I lived in a small town called Appleton until I was seven years old."

"When your mom died."

A curious uncertainty mingled with the sadness in his eyes. Was there something he wasn't telling her?

"Right. Then Dad brought me and my younger sister and brother back here. I grew up in the city for the most part."

Was this a good opening to inquire about the somewhat strange situation with a twin he'd mentioned before? Not normally nosy—she tried to show others the same consideration she desired from them—she nevertheless found what he'd earlier alluded to intriguing. Or maybe she was too quickly coming to find anything to do with Grayson Wallace intriguing.

He shifted his weight. "So, do you want me to stop by again tomorrow?"

"Would you?"

His brows knit together. "Three-thirty okay again?"

"I'll let Billie Jean know."

At the mention of Billie Jean's name, the corners of his

eyes crinkled. "I made sure Cory and I stayed here in the front yard so she wouldn't worry about us. But she'd frequently pass by the window keeping an eye on things."

Elise suppressed a smile. While Billie Jean was protective of Cory, keeping a close watch on Grayson Wallace might have more to do with the law-enforcement officer's athletic build than her friend's mother-bear tendencies. But she'd keep that hypothesis to herself. The good-looking bachelor probably already had an ego twice as big as his home state.

"Billie Jean thinks of Cory almost like family."

"I could tell."

Her face warmed as he studied her thoughtfully. She bent to pick up the empty tumblers, stacked them inside each other, then straightened to tuck them under her arm. Her gaze again met his.

"Thanks again for coming. And for the pizza. Sometimes it's hard at the end of the day to dig up the energy to cook."

"I'm the king of takeout." A boyish smile surfaced. "Not much fast food, but calling ahead to a decent restaurant and picking up a full meal on the way home."

Must be nice.

Maybe someday—when Cory was twenty or thirty—she'd try it herself. With effort she pushed aside the disheartening thought, refusing to get sucked into negativity. That was always a danger when she was tired, which seemed to be most of the time these days. She'd endured a sleepless night praying about Cory. Then all day repeatedly beat herself up over running to a policeman to save the day with her son. She hadn't been thinking straight when she'd met with Grayson last night—yet this evening here she was encouraging him to come again.

Grayson picked up the pizza box from the concrete steps and handed it to her. "Keep the leftovers. Might make a good lunch for you or Cory if warmed-up pizza is your style."

"Cory will eat it hot or cold." She tightened her grip on

the box and motioned to Grayson's injured arm. "I've been meaning to ask you what you did to yourself."

"It wasn't the outcome of, shall we say, one of my more graceful moments. Dislocated my shoulder."

She broke into a teasing smile. "Jungle gym? Tree climbing? Skateboarding?"

The laugh lines around his eyes creased. "How about leaping off a second-story balcony and landing on the hood of a car?"

"Ouch. Do you make a habit of that kind of thing?"

His grin broadened. "Only when bad guys are shooting at me."

A knot tightened in her stomach, and something in her expression must have given it away, for Grayson sobered immediately.

"I'm sorry. I didn't mean—that was thoughtless of me."

She took a rallying breath. "It's okay. Don't worry about it. So you're still on duty, even with the injury?"

"I'm confined to a desk and community work. Going stir-crazy, too. I've also been undergoing torture by a physical therapist for the past month to avoid surgery."

"Sounds bad."

"As dislocations go, it could have been a lot worse," he said with a grateful smile. "The sling keeps me from forgetting not to overextend myself. I should be back in business by the end of this month, first of next."

"Physical therapists can work wonders. When I was a kid, my dad tore his rotator cuff. Had surgery, then physical therapy to regain mobility. As a kid I found the whole thing fascinating."

"So let me guess—you grew up dreaming of being a physical therapist."

"I did, but then I got married right out of high school—" against her parents' wishes "—and Cory came along. Right now I'm taking general ed courses online, hoping that will give me an edge when I'm able to go to a real classroom."

He cocked a brow. "Working full-time, single parenting and studies. You have a lot on your plate."

"I can handle it." She squared her shoulders, determined that by God's grace she would. But how would she deal with classes and hands-on training when those came into play? Working part-time wasn't an option—and the thought of venturing out for night classes filled her with anxiety.

Concern lingering in his eyes, Grayson nodded. "I'll see you tomorrow, Elise."

She watched him to his vehicle, her throat tightening uncomfortably. Tomorrow would be the last day she'd allow him to spend with Cory. Yes, he'd willingly shared time with her son. Had reassured her Cory wasn't headed for a life of crime.

But his injury in the line of duty brought her up short. Someone had been shooting at another man she'd admitted into Cory's life. Encouraging a closer bond between the two would be poor parenting on her part.

No more cops.

Chapter Six

"Say again?" Gray kept his voice even, unwilling to betray the kick to his gut Cory's softly spoken words generated.

The boy booted a rock with the toe of his tennis shoe, sending it sailing toward the yard next door. He didn't look at Gray.

"Cory?"

The little guy's shoulders slumped, his body language clearly spelling out withdrawal. Resistance. But Gray waited. Cory wouldn't have said what he thought he'd said if the boy wasn't harboring something that needed to come out. If there was anything he'd learned as a cop, it was waiting things out even when you wanted to hurry them along.

Cory kicked at another rock. Grayson sent one sailing right behind his and the boy gave him a curious look.

"They yell stuff at her," he mumbled at last, now staring down at the ground with fisted hands.

"Who does?"

"Men."

Grayson took a few measured steps to close the short distance between him and Cory. "Do you know the men?"

He shook his head and kicked at another rock. Almost lost

his balance. But Gray steadied him, then crouched to place a comforting hand on his hunched shoulder.

"What do they yell?"

The boy's lips tightened. "Stuff. They drive by slow. Make kissy noises."

Stuff. It didn't take much guesswork as to what kind of stuff. But he had to make certain he wasn't blowing the situation out of proportion.

"Do you remember what they say?"

The boy gave a jerky nod. "I think it's dirty because Mom tells me never to say those words."

Gray nodded, careful not to betray his own growing anger. "What's your mother do?"

"She tells me to pretend I don't hear them and we get in the house fast."

Grayson picked up a rock, pitched it a few feet away. Then he handed one to Cory and watched him do likewise. The surprising force of the boy's throw undoubtedly reflected the degree of emotion within.

"When they yell at your mom, how does that make you feel? Mad? Scared?"

The boy's eyes flared defiance as he met Gray's gaze, but his lower lip trembled. "I'm brave like my dad. I protect my mom."

"I'm sure you do."

His jaw hardened. "I think Mom pretends she's not afraid. We don't go out at night. Not after those guys laid on the car. They—"

When his words broke off, Gray looked toward the street to see what had caught Cory's attention. Elise's vehicle had pulled in front of the apartment. As they watched, she got out and headed up the uneven sidewalk to stop in front of them.

She put a hand on her shapely hip. "My, but don't you two look serious."

Cory and Gray exchanged a glance, the boy's gaze warning him not to betray his trust. No wonder the kid wanted to punch out someone's lights. He needed to fight back, even if his anger was directed at those closer to his own age and size.

That explained a lot.

Gray rose to his feet. "Guy talk. Saving-the-world stuff."

She appeared unconvinced there wasn't more to the story, but she didn't make an issue of it in front of her son. Wise woman.

She turned to the boy. "Ready for supper, Cory?"

He looked up at Grayson. "It's tomato-soup-and-grilled-cheese-sandwich night. I have to get cleaned up. Fast."

A laughing Elise watched him charge through the four-plex's open door and take the steps up to the apartment two at a time. Then she turned toward Gray, her gaze sobering. "Everything okay? Neither of you looked real happy when I walked up."

"That looked like one hungry boy, so I won't delay you in getting supper started." He needed some time to digest what Cory had shared with him. "We can talk about it later."

Her flawless forehead creased. "That sounds ominous."

"You worry too much."

"For good reason." Her frown deepened, as if debating whether or not to push him for further explanation.

His cell phone rang and he checked the caller ID. Violet. He glanced apologetically at Elise.

"Go ahead," she mouthed as she moved away from him. "I'll wait."

He took the call, picturing his newfound sister. "Hey, Violet. What's up?"

"Am I interrupting anything?" A voice so similar to Maddie's echoed through his phone, but with a pronounced west Texas accent.

He glanced toward Elise, who'd set her purse and a soft-sided briefcase on the steps, then knelt to break off dead blooms from a potted geranium by the door. "I have a minute."

"I won't keep you long. I know it's only been a few days since you were here, but we're antsy for news. Any leads?"

"I'm afraid Dad isn't making himself easy to track by going off on his own instead of through a missions organization. I know he likes his independence, likes to follow God's leading on a day-to-day basis, but we'll have to talk him into rethinking that habit."

He'd do just that if—no, *when* they found him.

"With all the human and drug smuggling along the border, I can't help but worry."

"Don't go there, Violet. We all agreed to think positive about this—that Dad will be home by Thanksgiving like he planned." Despite his own concerns, he had to be the voice of reassurance. Worry and panic wouldn't lead them one step closer to finding Brian Wallace. "We're going to locate him and find out he shook off whatever ailed him. I know exactly what he'll say. 'Why'd y'all get so lathered up? You know the good Lord looks out for me.'"

Violet sighed. "I know God looks out for us, but people die or get sick or seriously injured every single day. Good people. Like Mom ending up in a coma."

She had a point. He couldn't argue with her.

"I can't pretend to understand all that's happened, Violet. But in the midst of the turmoil, you have to admit some good's come of it. We've all found each other."

"True."

"It's proof a higher power is keeping an eye on things. We can know that regardless of what happens, we have Him and each other. But Dad's going to be fine. I've known him my whole life. He's tough as nails."

"I don't understand why a father I never knew goes missing when we need him most—when Mom's bad off."

Or why he'd disappeared right when Grayson had determined to get to know him better, man to man. Or why a mother he never knew existed wasn't discovered until she was unreachable.

"I don't have the answer to that, either." He hadn't known Violet even a full two weeks and already he was her big brother, just like he'd been Maddie's all these years. Determined to protect her, reassure her. But he couldn't lie to her.

"I guess if there's no news…"

He sensed her reluctance to bring their conversation to a close. "I'll call as soon as I hear anything. In the meantime, you take good care of yourself and the rest of the family. Any signs of improvement in…our mother?"

Would he ever come to think of Belle Colby that way?

"The same." Violet sighed again. "You're coming this weekend, right?"

"Right. See you Friday." He shut off the phone and clipped it to his belt. Stood staring at the ground as the weight of the family situation increased tenfold. Like Cory, he had the urge to send a rock bulleting across the yard.

"I couldn't help but overhear." Elise's gentle voice penetrated the fog gathering in his head. "Your father is missing?"

"We've lost track of him is all." Downplaying it reassured himself. Helped him deal with it. "That was one of my sisters, Violet. The new one. Both my sisters tend to worry."

Elise, a shadow of concern on her delicate features, moved closer and he found himself sorely tempted to open up about the disturbing turns his life had recently taken. His siblings had the support of each other at the ranch, but he faced it alone, hundreds of miles from the rest of his family.

"He's a doctor who does a lot of short-term mission work in remote locations," he heard himself saying. "We learned he'd left his cell phone behind at one location, but that wasn't a cause for alarm until a few weeks ago when we found out he's been ill. My brother Jack went down to Blackstone, Texas, along the Mexican border where he'd last been seen, but couldn't find him. So naturally, we're more concerned now."

"I'm so terribly sorry." Elise placed her hand lightly on his arm, but the concerned expression in her eyes was immediately followed by one of puzzlement. "And did I also hear you mention your mother? That would be a stepmother, I assume? Has something happened to her, as well?"

How was he going to explain it in a way that would make any sense? He hadn't come to terms with it himself. "As unbelievable as it sounds, Sharla Wallace—the woman who died, the one I grew up thinking was my birth mother— well, wasn't."

She blinked. "You're kidding."

"I wish I was. We just learned that our dad and his first wife—our biological mother, Belle—divorced when we kids were tiny, each taking a boy and a girl with them. Dad took Maddie and me. Belle took Jack and Violet. They split up two sets of twins."

"Why would they do that?"

He met her horrified gaze, relieved to discuss the troubling situation with someone he could trust. "That's something we don't have answers to yet. Like I said, Dad's missing, then Belle Colby—my birth mother—fell from a horse several months ago and has been in a coma ever since. So we can't fill in the missing pieces."

"Oh, my goodness." Eyes wide, Elise momentarily pressed her hand to her lips, looking almost as overcome as he'd felt when he first heard the news. "I can't even imagine what a shock this must have been to you. But how did you and your siblings find each other?"

"As they say, it was a God thing." He glanced skyward, marveling at the whole turn of events. "In July Violet was in Fort Worth, hoping to find information about her father— my dad, whom she and our brother Jack knew nothing about.

She 'accidentally' met Maddie's ex-fiancé when he thought she was Maddie, and things took off from there."

"This is amazing."

"It is, isn't it? I have an identical twin, but no memory of him or of another little sister. No memory of my birth mother."

"Quite honestly, Grayson, I'm overwhelmed, as I know you must be. I don't mean to sound judgmental, but I can't imagine what would ever persuade parents to do something like that. I could never have given up a twin of Cory's."

He met her distraught gaze. "That's weighed pretty heavily on my mind, too."

"So instead of two of you, there are four."

"Five, actually." He couldn't help but smile as her eyes widened further. "Maddie and I have a baby brother, Carter, who is in Afghanistan right now. But he's definitely the child of Dad and the woman I grew up believing was my birth mother."

"I don't know what to say, Grayson."

"Not a whole lot anybody *can* say. But I appreciate your concern. You're the first person outside the family that I've talked to about this."

"I understand why you haven't. This is a lot for you to work through. With your father missing and your—" Her eyes sought his.

"Belle."

She nodded in understanding. "And with Belle being comatose..."

"Right."

"So she remarried and raised your brother and sister on a ranch in the west part of Texas?"

"She didn't remarry. That's another mystery. She, Jack and Violet go by the name Colby. Where did that name come from? We have a lot of gaps to fill in. That's one reason I'll be heading back to the family ranch on Friday night."

"A *ranch?* Your family has a ranch?" Cory was back, standing in the apartment building's open doorway, eyes bright with excitement. "With horses and cows and everything?"

"That's right." Gray shifted from the serious topic to one more suitable for the boy. "A big spread."

"Can I go with you to see it, Officer Wallace?"

"Now, Cory…" Elise moved to her son's side and ruffled his hair, but her gaze remained on Grayson, still cognizant of the gravity of their unfinished conversation.

"But I want to see it, Mom."

It might be the ticket to get the kid's mind off policemen. But admitting the boy into his private life wouldn't be the best move. Besides, he'd have to take Cory's mother along, and with all the upheaval in the family it wasn't a good time for outsiders—or explaining to his siblings his connection to this attractive woman and her son.

"We don't invite ourselves to other people's homes." Elise gave Gray a reassuring glance, communicating that she'd handle turning down her son's request.

"But it would be cool, Mom. I could wear my hat."

"You can wear the hat here."

"Awww, Mom." Shoulders drooping, he turned back toward the stairs once more.

When he'd disappeared, Elise resumed where they'd left off. "I'm terribly sorry to hear of your family's heartbreaking situation, Grayson. I'll pray for Belle's recovery and that your father will be found soon."

"Thanks. Much appreciated."

Cory again appeared in the doorway, his eyes glued to his mother with a pointed look. "Don't forget, Mom."

"Forget what?"

"You know." He jerked his head in Grayson's direction.

"Oh." A look of fleeting dismay crossed her features as remembrance dawned. "No, I won't forget."

Cory shot a quick, excited look at Grayson, then dashed up the stairs once more. Gray gave Elise a curious look.

She picked up her purse and briefcase from the step. "He's going back to school tomorrow and I promised him that if all goes well for the rest of the week, he can invite a friend for supper Friday evening."

"That should motivate him. He has a best buddy in mind?"

"Ohhh, yes." She looked none too happy.

"What's the catch?"

"You. You're the buddy he wants to join him for supper."

He chuckled, then thought better of it considering she didn't look thrilled at the prospect. "You're kidding, right?"

"Nope. He has his heart set on it. But it sounds like you already have plans for Friday evening."

He should hit the road to Grasslands right after work that night. Despite his relief at having someone to talk to about his situation, it wasn't a good idea to get further entangled with this little family. He already found himself too often thinking of Cory and his mother. Too often indulging in wishful thinking that could come to no good end.

Why'd she have to be the widow of a cop, anyway? And have a kid?

But…coming over that night might give him sufficient time to decide how to broach what Cory had shared with him. Give him a chance to talk to Elise about the likely source of her son's anger. The insight would give her something concrete to take to a professional counselor. Then he could step back before he got snarled up in another Jenna-and-Michael situation.

He continued to gaze down at her beautiful upturned face. Her dark, questioning eyes. *Lord, who am I trying to fool?* In spite of his best efforts, he'd already let himself get tripped up. He didn't want out of her life. Or Cory's. Quite the opposite. Maybe if he had more time…maybe if she had an opportunity to get to know him better…

"Supper Friday night? If that's what Cory wants, you can count on me to be there."

Her delicate brows rose, as if taken aback that he'd accepted. Given her aversion to lawmen, he hadn't expected she'd indulge her son's request to invite a cop in the first place.

But she had.

And he intended to make the most of it.

"Whooeee, honey." Billie Jean Danforth leaned her skinny, forty-something self against Elise's kitchen countertop, her blue, spiky-lashed eyes dancing. "He's one sweet-lookin' man, from what I've seen. If I wasn't devoted to my Roy, I'd be lookin' to see if he has any brothers."

"He does. A twin, apparently." Elise laughed at the astonishment on the freckled, bleached-blonde's face. What would she think of the rest of the family situation Grayson had found himself in?

Billie Jean hooted again. "The good Lord put two of them on this planet? I may have to rethink things with Roy."

Elise checked the clock. Six-fifteen. That "sweet-lookin' man" could be walking through her door within half an hour. Too bad Roy was working late at the mechanic shop a few miles down the road. Maybe he could lure Billie Jean out of here so Elise could have a few private minutes to make herself presentable. It wouldn't do for her friend to think she was "dollin' up" for Grayson. After all, she'd been forced to stress more than once since Cory blabbed the news of Gray coming, that the invitation was issued strictly at Cory's request. A reward for his good behavior in school the past few days.

Not that Billie Jean was buying any of it.

But it certainly hadn't been her idea to invite him. She'd even tried to talk Cory out of it before issuing the invitation, but he'd insisted Officer Wallace was his number one choice. She didn't want to renege on her promise and had been counting on Grayson not accepting to get her off the hook. Why hadn't he turned her down? Did he think, as Billie Jean was inclined to, that the invitation was from the mother rather than the son?

She'd worried for days that might be the case.

"He's a meat-and-potatoes man, I take it." Her friend sniffed the suppertime aroma appreciatively.

"I'm hoping so. Cory picked the menu." Thank goodness for slow cookers, or Gray would be having Cory's other favorite, grilled cheese sandwiches.

"Did he, now?" Billie Jean folded her arms and watched as Elise finished setting the table for three. "I do have to say I'm pleased—but surprised—that you're takin' up with another officer of the law."

Elise sighed with exasperation. "I'm *not* taking up with him. How many different ways can I say it?"

Billie Jean pursed her lips. "Let's see. He was here Friday afternoon. Sunday night. Tuesday and Wednesday. Now Friday. Looks like takin' up to me."

"Well, it's not."

"All I know is what I see with my own two eyes. I haven't seen that kind of sparkle in *your* eyes since you walked into this place over eighteen months ago." She motioned to the festively arranged table. "And this is the first I've seen *anything* like this coming out of you."

So what? She seldom had company. Never got to use her stoneware dishes, woven placemats and brass candlesticks. The table settings had been a high school graduation present from her grandmother. Even with money tight, she'd refused to part with them for a fraction of their value at a garage sale.

"Cory thought candles would be fun."

"Uh-huh."

Elise stared at the table, her spirits plunging. Would Gray think she'd gone overboard? Would it make him uncomfortable? Or worse—would it give him the impression she'd taken an interest in him? Maybe she should strip the table and start again. Bring out the plastic and other everyday durables. The paper napkins.

She reached toward one of the unlit candles, but Billie Jean materialized at her side and took hold of her arm.

"Come on, girl. Put that back where you had it. I'm giving you a hard time. Just teasing. I think it's great that this guy's helping Cory." She grinned. "And it's nice that Cory's old enough to appreciate it. So lighten up."

Lighten up. Easier said than done with the clock ticking away the minutes until Officer Wallace's arrival. All day she'd debated how to handle her son's growing affection for the police officer. In retrospect, giving in to inviting him tonight wasn't the wisest move.

But until they'd unearthed the source of Cory's anger issues, could she afford to cut ties with Grayson?

Chapter Seven

"Howdy, Cory."

As the boy in the cowboy hat eagerly let him into the apartment, the smell of roast beef and warm bread of some variety set Grayson's mouth watering. His eyes readily found Cory's mom busy in the kitchen.

The way to a man's heart...

But he didn't need a taste of her cooking to know he was already sliding down a slippery slope. He was a cop. He'd wanted to be a cop ever since hearing people talk in admiring tones about how a policeman had freed his little sister from the backseat of the remnants of a car crash that killed their mom.

He'd tossed and turned half the night, but still hadn't a clue as to how to get past the "no cops beyond this point" warning tape stretched across Elise's heart. How could he get to a place where his being a cop wasn't a constant reminder of her husband's death? He'd have to be cautious with Cory. Make no promises he might not be able to keep. But by giving in to Cory's pleadings to have him over for supper, could Elise be lowering her guard?

Maybe she'd give him a hint tonight.

"Come on in, Grayson. Supper's almost ready." Her welcoming tone drew him farther into the apartment as Cory almost danced around him in excitement.

"Smells mighty good." He caught and held her gaze, then she quickly looked away to turn off the oven. Almost as if nervous to have him here. Could it be that she hadn't entertained a man in her home since Duke's passing?

For some odd reason the thought kindled hope.

Not knowing what to expect of her decorating style, he was nevertheless taken aback at the sparseness of the furnishings as he crossed the living room to the kitchen-dining area. It was almost reminiscent of his college days when he and half a dozen other guys rented a house a few blocks off campus. Sleeping bags on the floor. Clothes, towels and shoes lined up around the perimeter of the shared bedrooms. Who needed dressers? Talk about a barren bachelor pad.

Her place wasn't quite as bad as that. But close.

Despite the minimalist furnishings, the place was neat and immaculately clean—unlike his undergrad residence. A table had been set with navy blue placemats, glazed white dinnerware and navy-and-white-checked cloth napkins. Candles, too, their gentle flicker casting a homey warmth. His mom—Sharla—had been fond of candlelight. His dad said she thought it made every meal, even something straight out of a can, special.

Cory set his hat on a corner of the countertop, then pulled out a dark oak chair and plopped down to gaze at the laden table. Beef on a platter surrounded by chunked potatoes, onions, celery and carrots. White rice. Drippings gravy in a spouted server. Green beans. Fried okra. Biscuits.

"Isn't this incredible, Officer Wallace? Roast is my favorite."

And apparently a rarity in this household from the kid's awed voice and wide-eyed reaction.

"Please have a seat, Grayson." By her anxious gaze directed at Cory, it was obvious Elise didn't want him further betraying their meager circumstances with his innocent comments. What had happened, anyway, to bring mother and son to this part of the city? An honest cop might not roll in dough, but surely her husband had at one time provided a decent home. Furniture. Sufficient insurance coverage.

What had become of it?

He settled in across from where he anticipated Elise would sit—likely closest to the work area of the kitchen—with Cory on his left. She looked lovely tonight in jeans and a high-waisted, flowing top. A delicate silver chain with a turquoise pendant filled in the V-neck, and her hair was loosely clasped at the nape of her neck.

A vision like that sure got a man thinking about what it might be like not to come home to an empty condo every night. Drawing his gaze from her graceful form, he chatted about school with a squirming Cory until Elise finally seated herself and turned to her son. "Would you like to give thanks?"

The boy nodded, unfazed by the request as many kids might be. Grayson closed his eyes and bowed his head. Waited.

Waited some more.

Silent prayer?

He opened one eye. Cory had his hand outstretched toward him, his gaze patient as if dealing with a child not yet schooled in basic etiquette.

"You're not holding hands, Officer Wallace," came his whisper.

A quick glance determined that Cory's other hand was clasped by his mother—and her free hand, like her son's, stretched out to him across the width of the table.

"Oh. Sorry."

He turned toward Cory to accommodate the limitations of his sling and obediently grasped the boy's hand. Then, after a second's hesitation, he took Elise's. Fragile. Soft. Warm.

Holding it self-consciously in his own, it was all he could do to keep his focus on the childish voice enumerating in detail to their Heavenly Father all that he had to be thankful for.

Whatever troubles Cory might have adjusting to the challenges life had slung at him, clearly poor parenting didn't fit into the equation.

"Oh, and thank you, Jesus, for this awesome roast," Cory finished up. "And for Officer Wallace being so awesome, too. Amen."

Amens echoed around the table. Hands released, leaving his feeling strangely bereft.

Grayson cleared his throat and caught Elise's eye as he spoke to her son. "You know, Cory, if it's okay with your mother I'd be more comfortable if you'd call me Grayson. Or Gray."

For a moment, perceiving a slight lowering of a delicate brow, he thought she'd deny the request. After all, he was spending time with Cory in what was basically a professional capacity. Not a social one. His presence was merely supposed to nip in the bud any behaviors that might later lead to more serious issues.

But she nodded affirmation, and his heart lightened.

"I think that's fine. He calls his sitter by her first name, too."

Cory motioned across the table. "Would you please pass the biscuits, Officer Wa—Officer *Grayson?*"

Grayson and Elise exchanged looks of amusement, then he set the biscuit basket down beside the six-year-old before helping the boy spear a juicy slice of tender beef and ladle gravy onto fluffy rice mounded on his plate.

With a quick glance at his mother, who was distracted with serving herself, Cory snatched up a green bean with his fingers and popped it into his mouth. Chewed. "Does your wife fix roast for you, Officer Grayson?"

Gray paused for a second, not looking at Elise but sensing

her listening to the conversation. "I don't have a wife, Cory. I'm not married. Never been married."

"Do you have little kids?"

"No. No children."

"How come?"

"Cory." His mother shot Grayson an apologetic look as she finished filling her plate. But Cory ignored her warning.

"Don't you want to be married and have kids?"

Grayson reached for a golden biscuit. Now there was a loaded question if there ever was one. "I'm not opposed."

"What's *'posed* mean?"

"It means I have no objections."

"What's no ob—"

"It means, Cory—" Elise gave her son a pointed look "—that if God wants him to get married, he will. Now let's change the subject, please."

Acquiescing, Cory poked a finger at a potato on his plate. "Did Mom tell you she's going to get me a pony?"

A forked carrot paused halfway to Elise's mouth. "Cornelio Tomas Lopez, I did *not* say I'm getting you a pony. And use your utensils, please."

Cory grinned down at his meal, undaunted, but reached for a fork. "Grandma said you had a pony when you were a kid, Mom. I need a pony so I can be a sheriff or a mounted policeman."

"Ponies are expensive. They eat a lot and take up a lot of room. They need a barn to live in, too."

The boy perked up. "We can fix the holes in the backyard fence. There's a shed if we can get Mrs. Morton and Billie Jean to take their junk out of it."

"No ponies." She turned to Grayson, shaking her head with an exasperated smile, and he guessed mother and son had been over this pony ground before. "So, Grayson, how is physical therapy coming?"

"Good—if I can take the therapist's word for it."

"Mom, did you know Officer Grayson jumped out of a window, and that's how he busted his shoulder? Is that cool or what?"

"Off a balcony," she corrected lightly, as if diving off one was an everyday occurrence, but a tiny crease between her brows surfaced. "I'm sure it didn't feel cool."

Gray chuckled. "No, can't say it did."

He deliberately hadn't shared with Cory any details of the close-call encounter when asked about the source of his injury. He kept under wraps that there were "bad guys" involved. He'd only inadvertently shared with Elise that gunfire had come into play.

Unlike TV shows and movies, that type of thing was a rare occurrence in the day-to-day life of the average police officer, although incidents seemed increasingly frequent these days. But the fact that it did happen and resulted in the death of Elise's husband—Cory's dad—made it a less than ideal mealtime topic. Nor could Gray discuss in front of the boy the issues that had been weighing on his mind since midweek when Cory had divulged concerns for his mother and told him about men making a nuisance of themselves.

Would Elise be willing to open up to him about it?

He cut her a quick look, a protectiveness welling up inside as she gently tucked Cory's napkin more securely on his lap. Regardless of whether his concerns were welcome or not, he wasn't leaving tonight until he got the full story from her.

"So what was this man-to-man conversation between you and Cory about the other day?" Elise kept her voice low as she walked Grayson down the stairs to the building's front porch. "The one with all the serious looks when I drove up."

At least her direct question relieved him of bringing up the subject on his own.

"If I tell you, you can't tell Cory."

"That all depends."

"Then it will remain between Cory and me." He needed to get to the heart of what the boy started to tell him the other day, but their relationship was still a fragile one and he didn't want the kid to think he couldn't be trusted.

"Excuse me? He's my son, and you agreed to—"

"Spy on him? Be a snitch?"

She folded her arms. He knew she was trying to appear forceful, but it was all he could do to smother a smile. She looked cute when she tried to be tough.

"I hardly think being a snitch is what I'm asking you to do."

"It's up to you. You want to know or you don't?"

Her lips formed a grim line, her gaze assessing him. "Okay. I promise."

"I think your fears are transferring to him."

A frown creased her forehead. "What do you mean?"

"Layman's guess, but I think he's acting out at school because it's a safe place to take out his fears for *your* safety. He told me he needs to protect you from men who make you afraid."

Her eyes widened as realization apparently dawned. "Oh."

"He says you don't go out much at night since, as he put it, 'guys laid on your car.'"

She slowly sank to the concrete steps, as if her legs would no longer hold her. He lowered himself down beside her.

"You okay?"

She nodded, but from her stunned expression he had his doubts.

"I tried not to let him know…not to react in such a way that it would frighten him. I thought I'd done that. He never talked about it afterward."

"What happened?" he asked gently.

A weary sigh escaped her lips as she stared across the darkened yard, the dim porch light its sole illumination. "Not long before school started, we'd gone to a Sunday evening church event. We stayed for the barbecue afterward and time got away from me. Cory was having fun with the games and the bounce house, so we didn't leave until well after ten o'clock."

She bent her knees and lifted her feet to the step on which she sat, wrapping her arms protectively around her legs, almost like a little kid might do. "The streets were surprisingly empty that night. Not much traffic. When I stopped for the signal at one deserted intersection, suddenly half a dozen men—older teens or early twenties—stepped out of the shadows of a closed shop and approached the car."

A muscle tightened in his shoulder as she paused, and he sensed her gathering the strength to continue.

"They surrounded us. Tried to open the doors. Pounded on the windows. Rocked the car. Made lewd remarks and gestures. A couple of them found it funny to stretch across the hood of the car."

Picturing the scene, he flexed his fingers as tension mounted. "What did you do?"

She closed her eyes momentarily, nibbling on her lower lip. "I said a prayer that there would be no oncoming traffic. And hit the gas. I ran the red light—and every red light the rest of the way home."

"Oh, Elise."

"The men jumped off the car by the time I got through that first intersection," she assured quickly, as if concerned he might think she'd harmed someone, "but I kept going."

"You did the right thing." Instinctively he knew she needed to hear that. "Did you call the police?"

She shook her head. "No. It all happened so fast. My cell phone was in my purse on the floor of the backseat. All I knew was that I had to get Cory safely home. I assured him everything was okay. Made him sing 'Jesus Loves Me' with me all the way back to the apartment. I got him tucked

into bed. Read him his favorite stories. Then after he fell
asleep—"

She shivered.

"Then what?"

"I went in the bathroom and threw up."

Without thinking, he slipped his good arm around her and
drew her near. She stiffened for a moment, then gradually relaxed as if drawing comfort from him as they sat in silence—
comfort he willed into her with every fiber of his being.

She'd been terrified. Thank God neither she nor Cory had
been hurt. But the experience had left a raw wound. No wonder she no longer went out at night.

"What about the other men?" He kept his tone gentle, as
he'd done when probing her son on the same topic. "The ones
Cory said drive by here and yell what he called dirty words."

She shrugged against him. "Neighborhood teens with not
enough to do."

"Except harass innocent women and children. How long
ago did this happen? Could you identify them?"

"Last week most recently." *Most recently? How long had
this been going on?* "I do my best not to look at them except
to keep an eye on where they are. I don't want to encourage them. I took Cory by the hand and led him straight into
the house."

She turned to Gray, her breath catching ever so slightly at
finding his face mere inches from her own. She looked away
at once, but his heartbeat ramped up to an erratic rhythm.

"I could probably identify one or two that I've seen before.
I don't think they mean any harm. When I've seen some of
them during the daytime, when they're not with their buddies, they're polite enough."

"I don't like the sound of it. If they come around again,
you call 911. You understand?" She needed to recognize the
potential seriousness of the situation.

"By the time the police could arrive, they'd be long gone.

Siccing law enforcement on them might encourage them to push things further. Retaliate. I can't afford to be known in the neighborhood as someone who's rocking the boat."

"What they're doing is against the law. I've already asked that police presence be stepped up." And he'd driven his SUV through the neighborhood last night to check things out himself. No sign of rowdy teens. "Sometimes all it takes is a cruiser making the rounds at unexpected intervals to get those types to move on. It's likely you're not the sole woman they've approached."

She turned toward him again, still secure in the breadth of his arm, her gaze uncertain. "So, you think this is what has Cory so angry?"

The situation made *him* angry, so why not a kid?

"Boys learn quickly that exhibiting fear isn't acceptable. But anger? One of the few emotions a man's at liberty to indulge in." He paused, drinking in the beauty of her dark, expressive eyes. Marveling at the gentleness of her heart and how quickly she was finding her way into his. "I think this tough front at school is a cover-up for what he's feeling inside, that he's powerless to keep you safe. He can't take on those men, but he did a pretty good job of straightening out those kids a few years older than him."

Elise uncoiled her legs, glancing down at her hands as she clasped and unclasped them on her lap. How he wanted to capture them in his own. Assure her everything was going to be okay.

"I tried not to let him know I was afraid." Her voice held a wistfulness that made Gray all the more determined to protect her and Cory regardless of risk of rejection. "I've been determined from the moment of Duke's death not to make my son a substitute spouse. Not to involve him in grown-up decision making or burden him with adult problems. I've seen too many single mothers do that. But it looks like my efforts have been in vain."

"Like I said before, kids are perceptive. I think Cory is remarkably sensitive and tuned in to what's going on around him."

She tilted her head to look at him, a faint smile playing on her lips. "Please don't tell me that trait will make him a good cop."

He responded with a soft chuckle. "Give it time. He'll eventually outgrow that policeman phase."

She bumped him playfully with her shoulder. "Promise?"

"Trust me." They sat in silence once more, listening to the night sounds. A cricket. Someone's television tuned to a weather report. A horn blaring from the freeway. A dog yapping.

He could sit here all night with her nestled beside him. Feeling her warmth. Breathing in the subtle rose scent of her. God *had* to show him how to bring her and Cory out of the hardships they'd somehow fallen into.

"Why are you living in this neighborhood, Elise?" His gaze took in his surroundings. The unkempt yards. Poorly maintained apartments and homes. The air of neglect and desperation that permeated the area. "Surely this isn't what your husband would have wanted for you and Cory."

She tensed at his words and instinctively he tightened his arm around her in a gesture of reassurance.

Abruptly she pulled away, the cooling night air rushing to fill the now-vacant space at his side. "Sometimes you don't get everything you want in life."

Her tone held an icy chill that cut him to the quick.

"No," he said, now cautious, "sometimes it has a way of handing us the worst when we least expect it." Didn't he know it, with the discovery of a mother and twin brother he'd never known, his dad missing, and the speculation that his dad might not be his biological father? Life had treated Elise less than kindly. He had to make her see that the down-hill slide she found herself on didn't have to continue. He could help her find a way out. "When it comes to your and Cory's safety—"

"It may not seem so to you, but I'm doing the best I can." Elise stood and moved to the apartment building's door.

He stood as well, searching her distraught gaze in the dim light. Kicking himself for mishandling the situation. "Elise—"

He stretched out his hand, but she stepped back.

"Good night, Mr. Wallace. Have a safe trip to see your family. And thank you again for spending time with my son. I believe I now have the answers I need to deal with the situation on my own."

Chapter Eight

What was wrong with her?

Remembering too vividly the warmth of Grayson's embrace and the concern in his eyes, she let herself into the upstairs apartment with a shaky hand. He'd startled her when he first put his arm around her, but after a few moments, when he made no further movements of a more intimate nature, she'd taken it for what it was. An act of comfort. Caring. But to her shame, she'd melted into him. Craving his strength. His warmth. The safety that emanated from him.

Once inside, she locked the door behind her, then slid the chain into its bracket as if to bar herself and Cory from the tumultuous past, the uncertain future—and from Grayson, who effortlessly drew her heart and hopes to himself.

In spite of Duke's betrayal, she still loved her husband. Still guarded his reputation and was determined that family and friends never learn what she'd discovered. But she hadn't counted on Cory idolizing him. At what point did she tell him the truth about his father—if ever?

In spite of his taking an interest in Cory's welfare, she couldn't even admit the true situation to Gray tonight. She'd all but slammed the door in his face when he'd verbalized his understandable questions about her meager circumstances.

Voiced his concern about her and Cory's safety in the neighborhood.

While she appreciated him spending time with Cory and figuring out what might be the source of her son's anger, the truth couldn't be shared. She couldn't betray her husband's trust.

He should have kept his hands to himself last night. He had no business slipping his arm around her. That last thoughtless squeeze…or maybe the prying questions…had sent her running up the stairs as if her dainty feet were on fire.

She'd made it abundantly clear he wouldn't be seeing Cory—or her—again. She had the answers she needed to see to the welfare of her son, and that was that.

It was his own fault.

"Earth to Grayson."

He jerked his thoughts back to his two sisters seated around the breakfast table at the Colby Ranch on Saturday morning.

"He's not usually this spacey, Violet. Must have something pretty intriguing on his mind." Maddie cut a look in his direction. "Or at least *pretty*."

Grayson noted uneasily the curious gleam in the eyes of both sisters. "I'd say thinking through how to find Dad is serious business, wouldn't you?"

Maddie and Violet exchanged a chastised look. Then Maddie stood, gathering the breakfast dishes since their cook/housekeeper Lupita had the day off. "Do you have any leads at all, Gray?"

"Investigative work is time consuming and methodical. It's not like on TV." He downed the remainder of his orange juice. "I took a couple of days off this week to continue calling hospitals, clinics, churches and police departments within a two-hundred-and-fifty-mile radius of the region where we think Dad may have gone. I'll do more of that this coming week."

He rose and carried his empty plate, glass and utensils to the sink where Maddie rinsed dishes and loaded the dishwasher.

"I realize the rest of you've done that on a smaller scale," he continued, "but it doesn't hurt to check again. Things can change from one day to the next, and giving my name with an 'officer' in front of it usually helps people remember better."

"I imagine so." Violet cracked a smile. "That would sure get my attention. You filed a missing person's report for us, so tell me again why that hasn't turned up anything?"

Gray leaned against the kitchen counter and folded his arms. "To be honest, that probably did little more than document our concern that we can't find him. It doesn't make him Amber Alert material. You won't see it on the ten o'clock news or find his face on a milk carton. Law enforcement doesn't have the resources to beat the bushes for a misplaced adult. Grown-ups go missing every day and most eventually turn up."

"But we think he may be sick. You'd think that would light fires under someone."

"What's working against us is that Dad isn't expected back until Thanksgiving, so he's not technically missing. If he hadn't left his phone behind in Blackstone, it would be a nonissue. The only evidence that he might be in trouble is a few people saying he appeared ill. While that alarms us, it's not an immediate danger kind of thing that would mobilize law enforcement. He's not suicidal or dangling from a ledge over the Grand Canyon."

"I know, but—"

"He's a grown man, Violet. A doctor. A missionary who frequently goes off on these solo journeys." He glanced at Maddie for confirmation. "The two of us know it's common not to hear from him for weeks or months. He gets busy. Loses track of time."

Violet sighed. "So we sit tight."

"It's going to be okay, Vi." Maddie dried her hands on a dish towel. "If anyone can find Dad, it's Grayson."

He wished she'd stop saying that. He could follow paper and electronic trails and track with the best of them, but there wasn't much to track. Dad hadn't used his credit or ATM cards in some time. Which made Gray uneasy. Very uneasy. But he couldn't yet tell the family what increasingly gnawed at the back of his mind.

What if Brian Wallace didn't want to be found?

He'd never have given that a second thought under different circumstances. But once he'd returned from his undercover assignment and discovered the family's—for lack of a better word—mess, it made disquieting sense.

Every single day, men and women walked away from friends and family and disappeared—at least for a time—in order to escape the pressures and responsibilities of their daily lives. Dad had harbored for a good long time the fact that he'd been married before. That he had more than the three kids who lived with him. Then there was the ugly question about paternity. Maybe the Wallace-Colby boys weren't even his biological offspring. Maybe he knew the secrets of a lifetime were about to break wide open and decided it was time to find an exit.

Their dad wasn't dumb. He'd taken his oldest vehicle on this trip—the one without GPS tracking capability. Then he'd conveniently left behind at one of his stops his state-of-the-art cell phone—the one law enforcement might have been able to "ping" for location coordinates. Troubling for sure, but right now he didn't need to give the family anything else to worry about.

"I'm doing my best, ladies, and that's all I can do."

Violet approached to slip her arms around him for a hug. "That's all we ask, Gray. Thank you."

Then she pulled back, mischievous sparks dancing in eyes so like Maddie's. "Now care to tell us what else—or *who* else—is on your mind?"

"Saw you sittin' on the front porch with Cory's cop last night." An early bird like Elise, Billie Jean popped open the door of the clothes dryer in the laundry room shared by the building's tenants. Pulling out an armload of bath towels, she motioned to Elise to put her own washer-damp bedding inside.

How much had Billie Jean seen? Grayson's arm around her? Her jerking away in childish panic when his question about the circumstances Duke had left her in to hit a nerve? Face warming, Elise stuffed the sheets inside, closed the metal door and selected the settings. With any luck, Billie Jean couldn't linger long to interrogate her this morning. She and Roy and the kids were heading out of town for the weekend. Leaving at eight.

Breathing in the nose-tickling scent of detergent, Elise relaxed against the vibrating dryer to watch her friend fold towels. "He was filling me in on what he'd learned about Cory's situation."

"Which is?"

"He thinks Cory's acting out at school because of me."

Billie Jean eyed her thoughtfully. "Bet that was a hard one to swallow."

"Not as hard as you'd think." Or at least not after she'd had more time to review the circumstances of Cory's school difficulties. "As much as I don't like it, it makes sense. Remember in early August when those men accosted us on the way home from church late one night?"

"Rocked the car and all that?"

"Yeah. And then you know how those neighborhood teens are always showing off to their buddies, pretending to be super macho and wolf whistling and hollering things out the car windows."

Billie Jean gave a self-mocking smile of regret. "Sad to say, that hasn't been a problem for me in recent years. But yeah, I remember you mentioning that."

"Grayson—Officer Wallace—suspects Cory's afraid on my behalf. Angry that he can't stop those men from bothering me. So he's acting out at school."

Her friend nodded as she folded another towel and added it to the growing stack. "Is this Grayson guy going to work with him? Help him deal with it?"

"Actually—" Elise tossed her long braid over her shoulder "—now that I know the source of Cory's outbursts, it's time to see if the school counselor thinks I should seek professional assistance."

Her friend gave a disbelieving laugh. "I think all the assistance you need comes packaged in that bighearted cop. He might not be a kid shrink, but it seems to me he's in tune with Cory. Far more than any professional would ever get. I can already tell Cory's demeanor has softened considerably from what it's been the past few months. Surely you've noticed."

She had.

Billie Jean folded a final towel and gave it a satisfied pat. "I'm surprised we didn't put two and two together earlier—connect it to that episode with the men on the street."

"Thankfully Grayson did."

"So…will we be seeing him again?"

"No." Still ashamed at the way she'd dismissed Grayson, Elise bent to pick up a ball of lint and tossed it in the wastebasket. "He's done what I asked him to do. Now he can remove his superhero cape and return to his real life."

"Superhero cape, huh?"

"That's what he called it."

Billie Jean's brow crinkled. "And you're going to let him walk away, just like that?"

"I have no reason to detain him."

"Honey, I can think of plenty of reasons to detain that handsome hunk of man. Your pride is gonna be your downfall. Never wanting to accept a well-intentioned offer of help. Always wanting to do everything on your own."

Her friend's words smarted. "Quite honestly, Billie Jean, it's not a good idea for Cory to get further attached to him. I appreciate what he's done for me, enabling me to better help my son, but it's best not to push a situation that could lead to heartache."

Billie Jean gathered up the towels in her arms, studying her a long moment. "Heartache for Cory? Or for you, Elise?"

"That house caught your eye, boy? It's for sale."

Grayson turned to an official-looking SUV that had pulled in behind his along the tree-shaded street. It was the sheriff he'd met last time he'd been in Grasslands.

"Hey, George." He stepped to the open passenger-side window. "I've always had an interest in early twentieth century Texas architecture. A sweet 1920s example like this grabbed my attention."

"Nice investment property—or a home if you're inclined."

Grayson glanced at the house situated on a spacious corner lot behind a gated, woven-wire fence. White frame with a charcoal roof and a wraparound porch, it was the epitome of Victorian flavor on a small scale. Came complete with an adjoining half acre or so of fenced garden space, a detached garage and shed. Admittedly, the overgrown yard could use some work, and Gray couldn't help but long to get his hands on it.

"Too far to commute from Fort Worth or to keep an eye on renters."

"But ideal if you join the sheriff's department. Takin' applications as we speak. I think that little lady I suppose you have back in Cowtown would love to call a place like this home."

Gray's mind flew to Elise as he pictured her seated next to him on the porch swing and Cory playing in the shade-dappled yard. Both the elementary school and the business district were a few blocks away. No traffic or crime to speak of. Kind of like the idyllic days he'd spent in Appleton as a kid.

But he wouldn't be seeing Cory again. Or Elise.

"Nobody's living in it," George persisted. "Been empty all year since Myrtle went to live with her niece in Lubbock. Call that number on the sign there, and Buster can let you in for a look around."

The police radio crackled. "The Colbys have long had a fine reputation in these parts. From what I hear, the Wallace name is the same. Just between the two of us, I have a feeling this deputy opening has your name on it."

Grayson cracked a smile. "You do, do you?"

The radio sputtered again and a dispatcher directed the sheriff to a stranded motorist north of town.

"Give it serious thought, son. And prayer if you're the prayin' kind." George lifted his hand in a parting gesture, then headed the vehicle down the street.

The job had *his* name on it? Not in a million years. Couldn't hurt, though, to give Buster a call just to take a peek at a fine-looking piece of architecture. But first he'd drop by the church to leave a few things Violet had given him for the office secretary. Sadie, was it?

In fact, he might have a chat with the local pastor. He'd met him during his first visit, and he seemed like a decent sort. Maybe he could help make sense of the chaos surrounding the Wallace-Colby clan in recent days.

As he opened the door to his SUV, he had second thoughts about driving. It was a nice day. He'd walk. Snagging a paper sack and tucking it into the crook of his good arm, he set out along the black-topped street. Although a warm, sunny day in early October, an undercurrent of autumn touched the air.

He soon found himself walking by the storefronts on tree-lined Main Street. Past Grasslands Coffee Shop and the Ranch House Bakery. Sally's Barbecue, Grasslands Bank and the Corner Drug Store. A little antiques shop. But what caught his eye well before he reached the four-way stop intersection was Grasslands Community Church, situated on a pecan-treed, small-town green.

It looked like a picture postcard with its white steepled frame. As he approached the modest building, he noted the neatly clipped lawn and the graveled path winding to the back where he glimpsed shrubs, rosebushes and flowerbeds. Seeing a white cross rising among crepe myrtles, he suspected the foliage might shelter a prayer garden.

Trotting up the painted concrete steps and through the white-painted door, he then stepped into the shadowed interior, the wooden floor creaking under his weight.

"May I help you?"

Grayson swung around to a young woman peering up at him through oversize glasses. Sadie, from the way his sisters had described her. Small and slightly built and not at all fashionably dressed, she nevertheless had amazing green eyes.

"Ma'am." He nodded and held out the brown paper sack. "I'm Grayson Wallace, Violet Colby's brother. If you're Sadie, she asked me to drop this off for you."

The woman made no move to take the sack. Her eyes flickered over him uncomfortably, not a look he was accustomed to getting from the fairer sex. Maybe it was the look-alike thing. He'd had more than one local give a double take when they spied "Jack" strolling down Main Street—with a haircut and minus the Western hat and boots.

"Yes, I'm Sadie," she said at last, although it didn't sound like she wanted to admit it. "Nice meetin' you, Mr. Wallace."

"Same here. But call me Grayson." He held up the sack. "Did you want me to put this someplace for you?"

"No, no, I can take it." She relieved him of the bag and set it on a nearby table, then stared at him with what could only be described as suspicion.

Okay. Apparently the old Wallace charm held no sway with this meek young woman. "Does your pastor happen to be in? Jeb, is it?"

Her eyes brightened, and Gray recalled his sisters mentioning they suspected the new secretary, who'd come to Grasslands last summer, was sweet on the preacher. Seeing her sudden glow, it sure made him wish he could put a gleam like that in Elise's eyes when *his* name was mentioned.

"The pastor is Jeb Miller. And no, he's not here." Her words had no more been uttered when her eyes rounded in alarm, as if realizing she'd admitted to a strange man that she was in the building utterly alone.

"Do you know when he'll be back?"

Her eyes darted away from his. "Any minute now."

"Do you mind if I wait?"

"You don't have an appointment…" she said weakly.

"No…but I hoped he'd have a few free minutes."

"You're the policeman from Fort Worth," she blurted, her tone almost accusing.

Small towns. "I am."

"You're moving here. Joining the sheriff's department."

He chuckled. "Not that I know of."

"That's good. I mean—" Her face flushed.

"Is my being here making you uncomfortable? I don't have to wait for Pastor Miller."

"No, it's not you. Not personally." Her hands made a fluttering movement. "It's just—well, police make me nervous."

"Nothing to be nervous about. Even in uniform, most folks think I'm a pretty good guy." He gave her his most winning smile. "Unless they're on the wrong side of the law, of course."

Her eyes widened. "I'm not suggesting you're not a perfectly nice gentleman." Her hands at her side made the agitated, fluttering motions again, almost as if readying for takeoff. "You see, when I was small, my father had a number of run-ins with the law. I know it sounds silly, but policemen are a reminder of that. The breakdown of my family."

"I'm sorry to hear that." He spoke gently, sensing this wasn't an easy thing for her to admit. "But from what I hear, you've found yourself a substitute family among the church membership in Grasslands."

He didn't mention the pastor's name specifically, but she blushed again. "I have at that."

"Well, what do you say I mosey on out of here and plan to catch the good pastor next time I'm in town. I'll call ahead. Promise." Goodness knows he didn't want to upset her fragile world any more than he had to. Violet hadn't exaggerated when she said the church secretary was a nervous Nellie.

He nodded a goodbye, then paused. "You mind if I take a peek inside the sanctuary?"

The fluttering again.

"I understand," he offered, to set her mind at ease, "that this is where my sisters plan to get married. My brother, too."

"Oh, yes. Certainly. Come this way."

He followed her through the double doors and stepped inside the hushed space, sunlight streaming from the tall windows illuminating rows of wooden pews.

Beautiful setting for a family wedding. Or three.

But why, in spite of circumstances to the contrary, did his inner eye envision Elise Lopez, gowned in white satin and lace, gracefully coming down the carpeted aisle? Her long hair draped over her shoulder. Yellow, beribboned roses clutched in her delicate hands. Sparkling eyes focused on him.

"In your dreams, Wallace," he muttered under his breath as the vision faded.

"Excuse me?"

His face heated. "Uh, sorry, Sadie. Talking to myself. Thanks for letting me take a look. Perfect place for a wedding."

He couldn't get out the door fast enough.

Chapter Nine

"Officer Grayson?"

He immediately identified the young voice on the phone, then glanced at his watch. Ten p.m. He'd just gotten home from the visit to Grasslands. "Cory?"

"Yes, sir."

He must have gotten the number from the business card he'd given him. But it was too much of a stretch to think his mother instructed him to call for a late Sunday night chat. Something must be wrong. "Is everything okay?"

"I don't know."

Elise's son sounded confused. "Tell me what you do know, Cory."

Even over the phone he could hear the boy inhale deeply, as if he had a lot of ground to cover.

"Billie Jean pounded on the door and woke me up. She was crying. Sayin' somebody broke into her house. Mom told me to stay here with the doors locked. She went downstairs, but it's been hours and hours and she hasn't come back."

Gray's shoulders knotted. "You're okay there? Doors locked?"

"Yes, sir. There's a police car now. I can see the lights."

"Stay right where you are, okay? Don't leave the apartment. I'm on my way."

Within minutes of securing Cory's promise, Gray was out the door and headed for the freeway. He'd said a cruiser was already there. So why had Elise not returned to her apartment? Hours, Cory had said. If he had his squad car, he could clear a path through the too-slow traffic and give the gas pedal the pressure his pounding heart demanded.

When at last he pulled up in front of the fourplex, a single squad car was still parked on the street, several handfuls of curious onlookers milling around in the yard. A quick glance confirmed Cory, silhouetted in a second-story window, had remained inside as instructed.

He wove his way among the bystanders to a spot in the yard where a uniformed officer was deep in discussion with Billie Jean and a man he assumed to be her husband. He spied Elise, off to the side in the shadows, and stepped in behind her to place his hand gently on her shoulder. Startled, she turned to him.

"Grayson. What are you doing here?"

He wasn't sure how receptive she'd be to his presence after Friday night's abrupt parting, but her voice held a note of relief, not opposition to his arrival.

"Cory called me. He said there'd been a break-in and that you've been away for hours."

"Hours?" She glanced at her watch. "It's not even been one."

"Apparently it felt longer to him." Gray tugged on her sleeve to move her well away from the inquisitive spectators. "So what happened?"

"Billie Jean, Roy and the kids were out of town all weekend. When they returned, they found the back door had been jimmied and was standing wide open."

"Did they lose a lot?" A family in this neighborhood

couldn't afford to lose much. Doubtful they'd have household insurance on any of their belongings.

"They took a DVD player Roy got her for Christmas last year and the laptop the kids do their homework on. A few other electronics." Items that could be quickly disposed of at a less-than-scrupulous pawn shop. "Billie Jean guesses their uninvited guests were mad about the slim pickings, so they trashed the place."

"You didn't hear or see anything?"

She shook her head. "No, but I'm a pretty sound sleeper."

"Any leads yet?"

"He's not saying much." She motioned to the police officer. "Mostly asking questions."

"Let me ask a few myself." Reluctantly, he left Elise's side to show his ID and confer with the officer. There wasn't much to share at this point. A routine breaking and entering. Theft. Closets ransacked. Drawers dumped.

Not nice, but it could have been worse had someone been home.

When he finished with the police officer, Elise was nowhere in sight, but he suspected she'd gone back upstairs to be with Cory. Within moments he was knocking at the apartment door, sensing when she confirmed his presence through the peephole—and her reluctance as she at last opened the door.

"Cory doing okay?"

She nodded and he noticed a weariness in her usually sparkling eyes. "It will take him a while to settle down but he's fine. I'm terribly sorry he called you tonight and you had to make a trip over here for nothing."

"I wouldn't say it's for nothing. At least *I'll* be able to sleep tonight knowing you two are safe."

Her gaze flickered momentarily to his and he gave her a reassuring smile—which she didn't return.

"Thank you." She took a step back as if preparing to close the door.

"Elise?" She wasn't going to like what he had to say, but he had to say it anyway.

She paused, eyes wary.

"Don't you think it's about time you and Cory got out of this neighborhood?"

Her chin lifted slightly, but she didn't look like she had a whole lot of fight left in her. "Didn't we have a similar discussion Friday night?"

"Not much of one as I recall. But I think this break-in warrants a reopening of the subject."

"Our home wasn't broken into. It's not likely to be since our apartment is on the second floor."

But the other night he'd noticed the back door accessed a minuscule deck. He took a step closer. "The neighborhood is deteriorating more quickly than it may have appeared when you first moved in. Now's a good time to start looking elsewhere."

"Thank you for your concern, but—"

"I can help you find something suitable." He'd recognized the unmistakable glimmer in her eyes. That independent don't-tell-me-what-to-do look. But surely she'd listen to reason. "I have the means to check out neighborhoods behind the scenes and confirm which ones are low-crime areas."

She gave him a tolerant smile. "I'm fully aware of where the low-crime areas are. But a move isn't an option right now."

His own chin jutted. "Pardon me for being blunt, Elise, but why not?"

Heart pounding, she stepped into the hall and pulled the door partially closed behind her. Cory was tucked into bed, but she didn't want to risk him overhearing.

"This is an affordable neighborhood, close to work and Cory's school."

"Get a new job. Put him in a new school."

He made it sound simple. Within reach. Made *her* sound dimwitted. He meant well, but he had no idea…

"Let me be blunt, too." She folded her arms to prevent him from glimpsing her shaking hands. "I have a high school education. No advanced degree. Outside of part-time jobs in high school, I have no experience beyond the year and a half at the clinic where I now work."

"You're taking coursework, though, right?"

"I'm a long way from a degree. In this economy, it's difficult to find a position that earns a living wage and doesn't involve night or fluctuating shifts. I need to work weekdays so I can spend as much time with Cory as possible."

"Commendable," he said with a brisk nod. "But where does his—and your—safety fit into the picture?"

"We're…we're trusting God to take care of that."

Was she? Was she *really?*

"I'm all for trusting God." Grayson's tone remained firm, but she sensed his frustration. "Nevertheless, He does give us a head on our shoulders. Common sense."

"I assure you I do have common sense. However, I can't financially manage a move right now. I'm hopeful for a raise after the first of the year. If that comes through, maybe I can look elsewhere. Besides, I'm also under a lease."

"A lease that's not keeping its part of the bargain can be broken." He motioned to the hallway's ceiling. "I suspect this place isn't even up to code. Do you see any smoke alarms? I didn't notice one inside the other night, either. The officer downstairs told me Billie Jean's place doesn't have deadbolts. I doubt yours does."

"I'm sure Mr. Morgan will install one now."

"All I'm saying is—"

"I know what you're saying." She reached for the door-knob. "I thank you for your concern."

"Elise—wait." He took a step toward her. "I'm trying to understand why the widow of a police officer lives in a place like this. I mean, I know the life insurance plan is decent. Surely at one time you had a home."

"Please, Grayson." She blinked rapidly, sensing a betraying moisture in her eyes. "I don't want to talk about this."

"If there's a hang-up with payout, a legal snafu, I can find someone to help you. The insurance company can be forced to make good."

"I know you want to help, but it has nothing to do with the insurance company." She gently bit down on her lip to stop its quavering.

She thought she'd been handling everything well since Duke's death. That she'd been a tower of strength for her son. But Cory had seen through that facade and had been negatively affected by it. With the home of her dear friend being broken into, the hopelessness of her own circumstances and her long-buried anger at Duke hit her full force.

Not only the anger, but the confusion. The guilt. The doubt that she even had enough faith to warrant God hearing her voice when she cried out to Him.

Please forgive me, Lord...but I've got to tell someone.

"It has to do with..." she cleared the lump forming in her throat "...my husband."

Gaze intent, Gray shook his head, not understanding. And why should he?

She leaned against the door frame to steady herself. "He... he had a considerable debt."

"Debt of a level that cost you your home, the life insurance pay out?" He stared at her in disbelief. "What'd he do, gamble it all away?"

She slowly drew in a lungful of air. "Yes."

Stunned, his gaze searched hers as the truth sank in. "But

surely…I mean, even if he gambled, there would have been something—"

"There wasn't. Trust me."

His hands fisted at his sides, his words taut. "You're saying your husband literally gambled your and your son's future away."

She hated hearing him put the ugly truth into words. But as she'd repeatedly reminded herself the past two years, Duke had no idea what he'd done to her. He never would have let it go so far had he known he'd leave this world before he could make things right.

He loved her. He loved Cory. But…

"He enjoyed horse racing." Her words echoed hollowly, as if coming from a great distance. "When he started going in the hole from lost wagers, he took out personal loans from the bank under the guise of other purposes. Then from friends and acquaintances—and others—to cover the loans. He got another mortgage on the house and—"

"Why didn't you stop him?"

Startled by the softly spoken accusation, her lips trembled. "I didn't know."

"How could you not know?"

She blinked back tears, her hand tightening on the doorknob as she turned to make her escape. She shouldn't have said anything. He didn't understand. He blamed her.

Shame washing through him, Grayson grasped her arm and turned her to face him. Tear-dampened eyes met his. Oh, man. He'd badgered her like a cop interrogating a suspect, and now he'd made her cry. What was wrong with him?

Before she could protest, he slipped his arm around her waist, pulling her close and wishing his left arm was unfettered by its restrictive sling. With a soft cry of surprise, she willingly melted into his embrace, her body trembling against the sturdiness of his frame as she sobbed into his shoulder.

"I'm sorry, Elise." He held her against him, warm and soft, but even in his grief at having pushed her over the edge, his heart hardened toward her husband. Some hero. Saved his buddy and went out in a blaze of glory, but he'd reduced his own wife and child to near poverty. Stolen their future. Possibly endangered their lives. What kind of man would do that to his family?

Minutes passed…and he held her. Just held her, his head resting against hers, her soft hair brushing his cheek. And he prayed. For her. For Cory. For what he should say—and shouldn't say. He'd already said enough to hurt her. As much as implied that her situation was her own fault. That she could have done something to stop her husband's downward spiral. He'd said enough to ensure she'd steel herself against him once she regained control of her shattered emotions.

He didn't need to suggest that if her husband loved her and Cory, he'd never have allowed this to happen. He might think it himself all he wanted, but he had no right to inflict that judgment on the woman cradled in his arms.

After an almost eternal stretch of time, she pulled slightly back and looked up at him. Uncertain. Embarrassed. For a long moment, they stared into each other's eyes. Silently communicating a mutual surprise. A curiosity. Attraction.

Hardly breathing, he could only gaze at her resting in the security of his arm. His chest rising and falling under her fingertips, he tilted his head and drew in a slow, anticipatory breath.

"Mom!" wailed a familiar, childish voice from somewhere deep within the apartment. "Where are you?"

"By the way, Maddie, have you sublet your apartment yet?"

Grayson had got on the phone first thing the next morning before he left for work, fighting his way through the haze that had enveloped him since the previous night. He'd come close to kissing Elise. Close enough to still feel the frustration of a longing unfulfilled.

Startled by her son's cry, both he and Elise had stepped out of the tender embrace. She'd frantically wiped at her eyes, then blew her nose on his proffered handkerchief before ducking back inside the apartment. Neither uttered a word.

He'd stood there alone in the hallway for a full minute. Dumbstruck. When had he ever let a woman rattle him like that?

"I'm not planning to sublet." Maddie's cheery voice echoed through the phone even this early in the morning. "Too much hassle for a few more months. Why? Are you fixin' to ditch your condo?"

He'd have to be careful here. Play it cool. "No, but through work I've learned that the widow of a fellow officer killed a couple of years ago is in need of temporary housing. Thought your place might be an option."

"Is this the one who saved his partner? I vaguely remember something about that. Big hero."

Yeah. Big hero, all right. "This is his wife."

"It's not a cheap apartment, Gray, being located close to the *Texas Today* office. I'm stretching myself to hang on to it for a few more months because I haven't wanted to mess with subletting it to a stranger and all the headaches that entails. I mean, what if someone damaged it and I lost my deposit?"

"I've met Officer Lopez's wife. She's a trustworthy and responsible type. You wouldn't have to worry about damage."

He could almost hear her thinking. Weighing options.

"You know, I'd actually appreciate someone keeping an eye on the place. If you know this woman to be a reliable sort, I'd even consider letting her stay rent-free for my own peace of mind. It's the least I can do for the wife of a man who put his life on the line."

And didn't lift a hand to protect his family's future.

"That's generous, but I can't let you do that. What if I

cover rent and utilities—October through December—
regardless of whether she's interested in staying there or
not? You're draining your savings right when you need it
to embark on a new phase of your life. Consider it a wedding present."

Maddie gasped. "Wow. That's an awfully generous wedding present."

"You're worth it."

"And you're the world's greatest big brother." The delight
in her voice brought a smile. "I can't figure out why a savvy
woman hasn't snatched you off the market yet."

He chuckled. "Maybe they already have a cool big brother."

"Ha ha. Very funny." She paused, then continued with an
unmistakable hint of curiosity in her voice. "So, I take it this
cop's wife is still single?"

Wouldn't you know it. Despite his best efforts, he hadn't
outmaneuvered her as he'd managed to do when she and
Violet had all but tackled him the last time he'd been in
Grasslands. Of course, Jack walking into the kitchen at that
moment had been what saved his neck. "Don't go there,
Mad."

"Just asking."

"She has a kid. Six-year-old boy. Need I say more?" That
was something he kept having to remind himself of. He might
be willing to go out on a limb for Elise, but a kid could get
hurt.

"Come on, Gray, you need to get over that. All single
moms aren't cop-a-phobic."

"Yeah, well, this one is. I'm keeping my distance."

Sort of. Maddie didn't need to know any details of his
tenuous relationship with Elise.

Or about the almost-kiss.

But he was determined to get mother and son to a safer
environment. It would take considerable sweet-talking to
pry her out of that fourplex and into Maddie's place. In the

meantime, though, he'd make certain she and Cory were more secure. He'd already arranged for a little surprise when she arrived home tonight.

Chapter Ten

Elise frowned. "I didn't call a locksmith."

A slim, capable-looking woman stood outside her apartment door early Monday evening. Dressed in jeans and a tan uniform shirt with official-looking patches, she held out a business card. *Rebecca Amerdin. Locksmith.*

"No, you didn't, but a certain police officer of our mutual acquaintance did. Grayson Wallace."

"Why am I not surprised?"

The locksmith smiled at the resignation in her tone. "As you probably know, there's no point in arguing with Officer Wallace. That's why I'm here to install deadbolts and check out your window locks. No charge. He also mentioned someone will be along in a day or two about smoke alarms."

Did that man's pushiness never cease? But she couldn't deny the flimsy locks would do little to deter someone intent on breaking in to the apartment. The lack of smoke alarms had made her uneasy for some time.

"He said you should call him when I got here so he can confirm I'm legitimate."

"You may as well come in then, Rebecca." She stepped back to admit the locksmith. Did the woman wonder what her connection was to Grayson?

"Please call me Becky."

While Becky set to work, Elise checked on Cory who was doing homework at the kitchen table. Then she slipped back to her bedroom, dug out a certain someone's business card and determinedly punched in the numbers. She needed to apologize, anyway, didn't she? For behaving rudely Friday night.

Her heart rate edged up a notch as she listened to the repetitive ring. She didn't want to talk to him tonight. Not before she knew what she wanted—or didn't want—from Grayson Wallace. She'd hardly thought of anything else all day except how she'd betrayed Duke's secret…and how dangerously close she'd come to letting Grayson kiss her.

Her breathing came unevenly at the memory as he came on the line.

"Elise. I take it the locksmith's arrived?"

The hesitation in his voice was instantly recognizable. Pleased that she'd called, but not quite sure what to expect. Was he regretting Cory's interruption last night? Or heaving a sigh of relief? Regardless, he had to wonder how she felt about it.

"Yes, thank you. It appears Cory and I'll sleep more soundly tonight."

"Good, good." He sounded more sure of himself. "Becky knows her stuff."

"Well, thank you."

"You're welcome."

"So…" She searched for something else to say. She should have taken a few moments to think this through, not snatched up the phone two seconds after the locksmith arrived. It had been her intention to apologize for her behavior Friday and for last night's outburst. To assure him she was fine and things were under control. He didn't need to hover protectively over her and Cory. But the only words that came to mind were *would you have kissed me if Cory hadn't cried out?*

"How was your trip to your family's ranch?" she ventured. So many times Gray's unusual family situation had come to mind. How awful it must have been for him to return from an undercover assignment to the astonishing news of family he didn't know existed and his dad's disappearance. "Any sign of your father?"

"Not yet. I'm calling around South Texas, checking out clinics and hospitals, but coming up empty-handed."

"I hope you find him soon."

"Me, too. Things are kind of tense out at the ranch, as you can imagine...but I did have a good laugh on Saturday."

The unexpected lightness in his voice pricked her curiosity. "What was that?"

"The local sheriff was at me again. Thinks I should apply for an opening there." He chuckled. "One of his deputies is retiring at the end of the year."

"What's funny about that?"

"Can you see me patrolling a county populated with cow towns about the size of a postage stamp? I mean, a few weeks ago the sheriff told me his grandma broke her leg chasing a calf out of her kitchen."

Elise giggled. "A calf? You're sure of that?"

"I did a double take on that one, too. But I later saw it in the local paper. C-A-L-F."

She liked hearing Grayson laugh. Could picture the corners of his eyes crinkling, his teeth flashing in a grin. Now didn't seem like the right time to tell him to hang up his superhero cape and leave her and Cory alone.

Her ears picked up on the sound of thunder rumbling in the distance. Much-needed rain? "I guess I should let you go. But I wanted to thank you for the new locks and seeing to the smoke alarms. That's very thoughtful."

"You're welcome. And while I have you on the line..."

She tensed. He wasn't going to bring up last night, was he? Surely he wouldn't ask more questions about Duke or allude to how she'd clung to him as if her life depended on it, her mouth only a whisper from his own.

"I was chatting with my sister today." Elise relaxed a fraction at the mention of his family member. "Maddie leases a high-rise apartment in downtown Fort Worth—not far from the *Texas Today* offices where she used to work. She's getting married in the not-too-distant future to a guy in Grasslands."

"Oh, how nice." Surely he wasn't going to ask her to the wedding.

"Yeah, great guy." He hesitated, as if not quite sure how to proceed—or if he should continue at all. "She happened to mention she's not subletting her place in the meantime. Too much hassle. It's standing there still furnished but without inhabitants until the lease runs out at the end of the year."

Was this heading where she suspected it might be? She couldn't afford an apartment in that prestigious part of town. Had he not listened to a word she'd said last night?

"Anyway, I mentioned I knew someone who might be in the market for a temporary place and—"

"Grayson. Stop." He was interfering again. "I know you mean well, but I can't afford a place like that. I thought I made that clear."

"Maddie would love to have someone trustworthy watching over it. For free. You'd be doing her a favor."

A knot bunched in the pit of her stomach. He'd bullied his sister into offering the place to her. A handout.

"Please thank your sister, but I can't accept."

"It would get you and Cory out of that neighborhood. Buy you time to make other arrangements. It would be a huge help to my sister, too."

"I'm afraid not."

"There are no strings attached, Elise." His voice had taken

on a more serious note. "I'll give you the key, help you get moved in, and then—"

"I appreciate your thoughtfulness. But the apartment here is close to work and Cory's school. Relocating would make for a long daily commute from your sister's place." Any second now he'd echo his earlier suggestion—that she get another job and put Cory in another school. "Please tell your sister thank you, but Cory doesn't need more upheavals in his life right now."

The firmness in her tone must have come across clearly, for he didn't argue. In fact, he didn't respond at all. Clammed up. She'd probably hurt his feelings. But with Duke she'd taken the easy way out by encouraging him to be the lone decision maker, the sole director of their family goals and finances, even when he'd hinted he'd appreciate her input. Her unwillingness to actively engage in those areas had set the stage for her own downfall. In her immaturity she'd abdicated her responsibilities as an adult—and look where that had gotten her.

Thunder rumbled again. Closer now.

"Grayson?"

For a moment she thought he would remain silent and let her hang up on him without so much as a polite farewell, but then she heard him clear his throat. "Did things go okay at school today? After the upset last night, I mean."

Why did Grayson have to be so kind? "Yes, he's fine. He got a lot of attention at school when he related the evening's events."

"You know, it's funny…" but he didn't sound as if he thought anything was funny "…after spending those days with Cory, I miss him now. I was glad he felt he could call me last night."

"Thanks for not being mad at him."

"Why would I be mad? I only wish I'd have had a few minutes to chat with him last night. Commend him for his bravery as he awaited your return." He paused. "So…you'll tell him hi for me?"

"I will."

"Thanks. And, um…good night."

She shut off the phone and sat on the edge of her bed, staring at the wall. He missed Cory. Cory missed him, too. If she'd be honest with herself, she missed Gray as well. Too often she found herself recalling those tender moments in his arms when she'd thought he was going to kiss her.

When, yes, she'd *wanted* him to kiss her.

Which was stupid.

It had been her foolish imagination that he might take a personal interest in her. But tonight made the situation quite clear. The locksmith. The smoke alarm. A free apartment. Grayson didn't think of her as a capable woman who'd endured setback after setback since the death of her husband. He saw her as helpless and viewed her and Cory as a do-gooder project like the ones Cory said Gray had told him about. The food bank. Men's shelter. The elderly neighbor whose car had a flat tire.

He'd probably have groceries delivered next. Give her a gasoline card. Not that she couldn't use them…

She balled her hands tightly in her lap. She wouldn't accept anything else from him. The lock on the door and smoke alarms would be the last of it. Billie Jean might scold about her pride, but pride was all that got her out of bed in the morning. All that kept her holding her head up and putting one foot in front of the other.

She wiped away a tear.

Pride was all that ensured she didn't curl up on the bed at this very moment and cry herself to sleep.

"So you see, Reggie, why I'm concerned. Professionally speaking, I mean." Grayson gazed solemnly at his fellow officer—and former church youth coach—as they finished securing a final load in the pickup. Monday night's thunderstorm had broken off a massive limb from an old oak tree in his friend's backyard, barely missing the house. Together they'd sawed the branches into more manageable lengths.

A grin split his burly mentor's ebony face. Twelve years Gray's senior, Reggie Lenard had filled a gap sometimes left vacant when Grayson's father had been immersed in his medical studies. "Professional concern, is it? Coulda fooled me."

Grayson slammed the tailgate into an upright position, hoping he hadn't gotten ahead of himself when he'd loosed his arm from the sling for a short while. He didn't relish admitting the source of any setbacks to the physical therapist.

"Keeping people safe is what I do."

"So she's pretty, is she?"

Gray shot his comrade a dirty look, but Reggie held his hands up in an innocent gesture, a grin widening. "Just makin' conversation."

"*Anyway,* as I was saying, it's a rough neighborhood. I hate seeing a cop's widow reduced to those circumstances, but she refuses my sister's apartment as a temporary solution."

Reggie pulled out a handkerchief and wiped the sweat from his forehead. "Sounds like a woman who doesn't need a buttinsky man ordering her around and telling her how to live her life."

Gray gripped the tailgate. "I'm not being a buttinsky. She *asked* me to help with her son's behavioral problems. I think they stem from concern for his mom's safety which, in my opinion, is at risk if she continues to live there."

"Free world."

"I'm asking for advice here, Reggie. Give me a break, okay? I don't want anything bad to happen to Elise and Cory."

The older man crossed his forearms and leaned back against the truck. "If the woman doesn't want to move, she isn't going to move. I'm not convinced she'll be easily persuaded."

Gray shook his head and Reggie chuckled.

"You should see your face. This lady's snagged your attention in a major way. The real issue here is how to get her to overlook that you're a cop, isn't it?"

Gray shrugged. That's what it boiled down to.

"She's a believer?"

"Yeah."

"That's in your favor. But I can tell you one thing for sure—she won't be keen to risk losing another man to a badge. You have to face it, this might be a whole different story if you weren't a cop."

Gray's gut twisted. That's the same conclusion he'd come to last night after he'd hung up from Elise's phone call. The one shot he had at possibly winning her over wasn't a direction he was ready to go. "Are you suggesting I resign from the force to win the fair maiden's heart?"

It sounded crazy to voice it aloud.

"Did you hear me sayin' that?" Reggie studied him with narrowed eyes. "Your perspective is getting out of whack. You just met this lady, yet you're all caught up in her business. Caught up in the way she smiles at you and makes your heart go pitty-pat. Totally ignoring the fact she's made it clear she has no interest in another cop."

"You think I should forget about her."

"That's not for me to say. Just keep in mind that you only have five years under your belt, but there's already scuttlebutt that you've got the makings of a stellar career. I advise you not to rush into anything. Give it serious prayer."

Gray tightened his grip on the tailgate, mulling his friend's words. He'd come way too close to kissing her, which would have seriously complicated things. And Cory had already wormed his way into his heart in record time.

"Don't take it so hard." Reggie's voice softened, his eyes filled with compassion. "From what you've filled me in on tonight, you've got enough to deal with as it is, what with your dad missing and all the rest. Thank the good Lord you didn't get as far into this as you did with Jenna and her boy."

"True." He'd dated Jenna for almost six months before things fell apart.

"Have you seen her and the kid since you've been back?"

"No." He'd almost called when he first returned, but something restrained him. God whispering, *"I've closed the door."*

"Better that way. She might have missed your sorry self and let you back into their lives. It wouldn't have lasted and you and the kid would have gotten hurt even worse."

Gray stared at the ground. "You know, with the Jenna thing and now Elise, I'm doubting it's realistic to have it all—a career in law enforcement and a thriving family life."

"Thinking negative like that isn't the way to go, Gray. It can be done. I'm doing it. But it isn't easy, I can tell you that." He paused. "It takes a special kind of woman to be the wife of a cop. Or for a man to be the husband of a cop, for that matter. Someone who's independent enough not to require a whole lot of handholding. Who is emotionally sturdy and has a faith big enough to deal with the realities of police work. You think this Elise is that kind of woman?"

Gray's memory returned to what he knew of her. How she was afraid to go out at night. How her fear had transferred to Cory. How she worried her son would get attached to another man who might meet an untimely end. How she'd broken down and sobbed in his arms the night of the break-in when she'd told him about Duke's gambling. "I don't know."

"Then get to know. Find out before you make decisions of a permanent variety." Reggie rapped his knuckles on the side of the truck and pushed away from it. "You stayin' for supper? Shana's making spaghetti. Homemade bread."

"Tempting, but I'm going to pass. Thanks."

"Isn't Sunday your night to host the gang for football?"

"Oh, right...." During football season a group of law-enforcement friends took turns sharing their widescreen

TVs—his one personal indulgence. It was always a high-spirited afternoon or evening of pigskin talk and barbecue with a dozen guys and gals on the force, some with significant others.

"Invite this Elise to join us."

Driving Elise farther away from him before he'd even come to terms with where he wanted to go in his career seemed premature. He'd only been on one undercover assignment. He'd been told he'd done well and he'd be getting another one in the not-too-distant future. But was that the route he wanted to go for the long term?

"Hours of cops and football might not be her favorite way to spend the afternoon."

"That should tell you something right there." Reggie turned to him, eyes solemn. "The right gal will come along, Gray. Don't force a square peg into a round hole. I tried to do it the first go-round and you know how that turned out."

Reggie's first wife couldn't take it. The long hours. Erratic shifts. The potential for danger each time her husband donned a uniform. His pal was right. Being married to the "wrong" person was a thousand times worse than not being married at all. He'd waited this long and, although it left his heart heavy, he could wait a while longer.

But why did God have to dangle the beautiful Elise in front of him right when he was getting settled into his career? Almost as if to force him to make a choice between the job he believed God led him to and a woman who would be so easy to love.

Chapter Eleven

"I wish Officer Grayson would come again."

Lower lip protruding, Cory crawled into his bed on Tuesday night. Elise sat down on the edge of it, pulling the sheet up to tuck him in. She'd let him stay up later to study the moon from the deck for his science assignment. There were few stars visible with the city's soft glow illuminating the nighttime sky. It was so different from Canyon Springs, an official Dark Sky City where the Milky Way plainly swept across the heavens.

"He's a busy man." She flinched inwardly at placing the blame for Grayson's absence on him, not on her own determination to keep him at arm's length.

"Can we invite him to supper again? I want to show him my math papers."

"He doesn't live close by." She gently brushed back his hair.

"But maybe he'd come if you told him about the As. He might want to see them."

He probably would. Grayson seemed to take an interest in whatever her son did, always giving him his undivided attention. He'd come running Sunday night when Cory called after the break-in. But didn't the fact that Cory had already gotten attached to him justify her decision to keep the two apart?

"Please, Mom? Can I call and tell him about my As? He says if I want to be a policeman I have to get good grades."

She wished Grayson wouldn't indulge that line of thinking. Didn't accountants need good grades, too? And dentists? "Like I said, he's a busy man."

"That's what you always say." He turned over and gave his pillow a vicious punch. Kept his back turned to her.

It had been a mistake to ask Cory's cop for help in the first place. What if Cory figured out that Gray coming into their lives had been a direct consequence of misbehavior at school and he decided to act up again? According to Miss Gilbert, there had been pushing and shoving on the playground this morning, but nothing major like the last time.

She placed her hand on her son's shoulder, but he shook it off, mumbling something into his pillow.

"I can't hear you, Cory."

He jerked the covers over his head.

"Cory." She hated when he got like this.

Abruptly he sat up in bed, his lower lip trembling. "I don't know why you don't like him, Mom. He's nice. I think he likes us."

"It's not that I don't like him, sweetheart." Her breath caught as she again recalled that almost-kiss. "I think he's nice, too. And yes, I think he likes us."

"Then why can't he come back? Billie Jean says he's sweet on you. Why can't you be sweet on him, too?"

She'd have to have a chat with her downstairs neighbor. "Honey, he came here to see *you* because he likes you."

"Doesn't he like me anymore?"

She was digging herself in deeper by the second.

"Of course he still likes you, but he—" He what? He'd taken her unsubtle hint that she didn't want him coming around anymore? That she didn't intend to allow the spark that had flared more than once between them to fan into a flame? "He has a job and his own family to take care of."

"But he said he isn't married. He doesn't have kids."

She drew in a slow breath, recalling how Grayson had shared with her the troubling events surrounding his father's disappearance and Belle's comatose state. "No, but he has brothers and sisters and a mom and dad."

"At that ranch?"

"Yes. And right now they need his attention."

"But when they don't need his attention, he'll come back to see us, right?"

Her heart ached at the hope in his voice. She'd have to give this more thought. Prayer. If she allowed it, there would have to be boundaries set. "We'll see."

"All right!" With a grin she loved, Cory gave her a hug, then plopped back on his pillow.

She once again tucked him in. Kissed his forehead. Then she moved to the door and flipped off the overhead light, ushering in the darkness. "Sleep tight."

Cory giggled. "Don't let the bed bugs bite."

She pulled the door closed and headed to the kitchen to finish cleaning up. *Grayson Wallace.* Only a dozen days ago she hadn't even known he existed. But in that short length of time he'd already managed to wedge himself into her life and that of her son. How quickly she'd come to look forward to his stopping by to see Cory. How easily she'd leaned into his shoulder for comfort. Fallen into his arms when overcome by the situation Duke had placed her in.

Surely there could be a happy middle ground. One where Cory could see Grayson on occasion, yet where she could keep her distance and wouldn't feel as if she was accepting charity.

She squirted detergent into the sink and turned on the hot water to fill the chipped basin. After a moment, she turned it off to better hear the sounds coming from the street side of the house. Cars revving. Whoops. Shouts.

The neighborhood had gotten rowdier and rowdier in recent months. If only…no, accepting Grayson's offer of his sister's apartment wasn't an option. He'd no doubt badgered her into making the generous contribution to his latest benevolence project.

She didn't like being considered needy in his eyes or her son viewed as underprivileged.

Nevertheless, she and Cory were safe now. Grayson's locksmith had seen to that. It was true that they'd become prisoners in their own home once the sun set. But that wouldn't be forever. She'd get her physical therapy degree as quickly as possible and begin looking for a new job. A new home.

Even though that was years away, a quiet hope surged inside her, overriding the raucous street-side noise. A verse from the Old Testament book of Jeremiah pressed in upon her spirit. "For I know the plans I have for you, declares the Lord. Plans to prosper you and not to harm you. Plans to give you hope and a future."

Today's circumstances wouldn't be forever. Things would change. Get better.

Reassured, she turned again to the sink just as the unmistakable report of gunfire and the sound of shattering glass jerked her back to reality.

Thank God she'd called him.

And thank God the bullet that shattered Cory's bedroom window lodged in the wall near the ceiling above his bed.

He was safe. Elise was safe.

That's all that mattered. That and getting her out of that place and over to Maddie's apartment.

To his relief, Elise hadn't argued with him when he told her where he was taking her. Too shaken to resist, she and Cory had sat quietly on their apartment sofa, wrapped in a blanket and each other's arms as the responding police officers concluded their investigation. A random, drive-by shooting. A stray bullet. Too many of those in the city these days, and this was just one more. All in a day's work for Fort Worth law enforcement.

Except this incident involved two people Gray had come to care for.

At his insistence, Elise had packed suitcases for both of them, her movements silent. Wooden. And now, with an exhausted Cory tucked into Maddie's bed for the night, she stood in the darkened living room, wrapped in his sister's afghan.

Watching her stare out the window at the city lights sprawling below, his heart went out to her as he recalled her quavering voice on the phone. Her ashen face upon his arrival. Her almost zombielike movements as she gathered her and Cory's things and allowed him to escort them to his SUV.

Not wanting to startle her, he spoke as he approached from behind with a cup of hot tea. "Elise?"

She turned toward him, the faint light from the window illuminating the weariness in her eyes. The uncontrolled shuddering that had tortured her for hours had subsided. But the hands that clasped the afghan around her shoulders remained unsteady.

"Maybe this will warm you up."

She secured the crocheted comforter and reached out for the cup. "Thank you."

She appeared so fragile standing there. Why hadn't he pushed harder Monday night for her to pack up and come to Maddie's place? She shouldn't have had to go through this. The terror of racing into Cory's room, not knowing what she'd find. If only he could turn back the clock and refuse to take no for an answer.

But what was done was done.

He offered what he hoped was an encouraging smile. "You might want to sit down before you fall down."

She shook her head, then turned back to the window, the steaming cup clasped in her hands. After a long moment, her words came softly. "I like looking out at the city, don't you? I can see why this place appealed to your sister. You're up here, above it all, where nothing down there can touch you. You're safe."

He took a step closer and hesitantly placed a hand on her shoulder. She flinched, but didn't pull away.

"I'm sorry about tonight, Elise."

He felt the sigh more than heard it. "You warned me. Now's your opportunity to say 'I told you so.'"

"I'd never do that."

She turned to gaze up at him, her eyes devoid of their usual sparkle. "Why not? You were right."

"You were doing what you thought best."

"I was…wrong."

The self-condemnation in her tone wrenched his heart. "Maybe. But you couldn't have foreseen what happened tonight."

"Cory could have been killed."

"He wasn't." He tugged the afghan more snugly around her shoulders. "You should call in to work tomorrow. Take a day off. Spend it with Cory."

"I can't. I have too much to do."

"You need to rest. Recover from the shock. Cory does, too. Do it, Elise."

She took a sip of tea, then set her cup on a glass-topped table. For several minutes they stood gazing out at the cityscape, watching the threads of traffic weave through the streets below.

"Since you've never explained why you haven't returned to Arizona, I have to assume you have your reasons. But you need to give serious thought to moving back home." Not that he wanted her to, but this was no life for Elise. She belonged in a small, safe town surrounded by friends and family.

Dark eyes filled with emotion, her words came softly. "I can't go back. Not yet."

"Are you on the outs with your family?"

"No."

"Then go home, Elise."

"I…can't."

He caught the break in her voice and turned her toward him, her face bathed in a soft glow from the windows. "Why not?"

"Because they'll find out…" She tightened her grip on the afghan. "They'll find out what Duke did."

"They need to know what's going on."

"I can't—he's their hero. He's the whole community's hero in many ways." She released a quivering breath. "Small-town boy makes good. Big-city cop saves his partner's life. I can't take that from them."

"You wouldn't be taking anything from them. That was Duke's choice when he did what he did to you."

She took a step away. "You still don't understand."

"Then help me so I can."

"Don't you see? *They'll blame me.*"

He frowned. "Why would they blame you? You didn't do anything wrong."

"Maybe I did." She paused. "Maybe I made Duke feel he had to provide way more than we could afford. Maybe he thought he had to give me everything it had taken decades for our parents to acquire—a home, furniture, nice cars."

"I can't see you ever making anyone believe that." But gazing into the face of the sweet treasure before him, he could understand why Duke wanted to give her whatever her heart desired. Only he'd gone about it the wrong way.

"Maybe I unintentionally expected too much. Then he

took a chance—gambled—in hopes of hitting it lucky and making dreams happen overnight."

"That's how a gambler may think, Elise. Look for a short-cut. An easy way out. But nobody makes them think that way."

"I wish you could understand."

He ran his hand along her upper arm. "I think I understand more than you think I do. Don't let pride keep you from going home. From going where it's safe. From going where you belong."

She stared up at him, bewilderment in her eyes. "Maybe that's just it. I don't know where I belong anymore."

Shuddering at the realization of how close of a call she and Cory had escaped tonight, Gray gently drew her close. Then to his surprise, he felt her hands splay across his chest and gradually snake up to his shoulders as she pressed in closer. The afghan slipped from around her arms, puddling on the floor, and she pulled back slightly to gaze up at him. Her eyes questioning. Longing.

Heart hammering, he accepted the invitation and lowered his mouth to hers.

Holding his breath, half expecting her to push him away, he tentatively brushed his lips against Elise's as he breathed in the intoxicating scent of her soft skin. Felt her press more closely against him.

She's only seeking comfort. Reassurance. Don't take advantage of that. But when she didn't resist his cautious caress, he couldn't help but adjust his arm around her and press his lips more fully to hers.

Elise. Safe in his arms.

Thank You, God, for protecting her and Cory.

After some moments, Gray slowly drew back, brushing aside the silken strands of the dark hair framing her face. Heart pounding, he gazed in wonderment at the lustrous brown eyes looking into his with quiet, confident trust.

It is not good for the man to be alone.... The words of the Book of Genesis pulsed through his mind. God created the lovely Elise he now held in his arms. A gift from God, one every bit as cherished by Gray as Adam had cherished his own gift of Eve.

But was she *his* gift?

Or was he, as Reggie had suggested, letting his perspective get all out of whack? *You just met this lady, yet you're all caught up in her business. Caught up in the way she smiles at you and makes your heart go pitty-pat. Totally ignoring the fact she's made it clear she has no interest in another cop.*

She didn't want a cop.

He was a cop.

He closed his eyes, resisting that painful truth. Prayer. That's what his pal had said would provide the answers. Prayer. But the only prayer he could utter was that these precious minutes holding Elise would never end.

"Gray?"

He opened his eyes as her gentle caress skimmed the late-night stubble along his jaw. Her questioning gaze probed his for a breathless moment. Then her hand once again slipped behind his neck and she drew his mouth back down to hers.

Early Wednesday evening, Elise glanced at the clock in the kitchen and her heart skittered. Almost six-thirty. Table by the window set. Salads made. Lemon chicken with rice simmering in the electric skillet. The sun would be setting shortly, the sky already a blaze of color streaking through the clouds outside the floor-to-ceiling windows.

Grayson would be arriving soon. In fact, he was late.

What would they find to talk about? Would they pretend nothing had happened between them last night? That the kiss was no more than a manifestation of the fear and stress of what they'd endured from the drive-by shooting?

And if he brought it up, how should she respond?

She'd followed his suggestion, explaining the situation to her employer and taking the day off. Same for Cory, who was not only over-the-top giddy about their temporary quarters, but repeatedly asked if Grayson would let them live there forever.

Billie Jean had picked her up midmorning and taken her back to the apartment to retrieve her beloved pink geranium from the front porch and the car she'd been too shaken to drive last night. Like Elise, her friend had been enamored with the apartment overlooking the city. "Like livin' in a dollhouse in the sky," she'd said.

Arms outstretched, Cory now stood by the broad expanse of glass where he'd spent much of the day. He'd endlessly oohed and aahed over the surrounding skyscrapers, the traffic surging below and the ever-changing play of light over the landscape.

Unfortunately, flashing lights from police cars were easily spotted from this elevation, which had triggered more cop talk throughout the day.

"This is the greatest, isn't it, Mom?"

"It is." A surge of happiness filled her as she joined him by the windows. But did that stem from the apartment itself—a haven of safety—or from the lingering effects of being held in Grayson's strong arms and feeling his lips move gently on hers?

Neither had said anything when they'd pulled back from the prolonged kiss. They'd stood gazing into each other's eyes, as if not quite sure how it had happened—or if it should happen again. Then she'd followed Grayson to the door as he'd quietly let himself out.

But he was a policeman…just like Duke. Surely God wouldn't bring another one into her life. And yet… Her heart scampered again at a knock on the door. Where had she gotten the nerve to leave a message today, asking him to join them tonight?

Cory raced to the door and managed to get the locks unfastened. Then he threw himself into the arms of the startled, civilian-dressed officer of the law. As she approached to welcome him, she detected the faint scent of a spicy aftershave. He must have cleaned up at the division headquarters or swung by home first.

"Mom fixed chicken, Officer Grayson." Cory clung to his friend, eyes dancing. His openness, his vulnerability, tugged at Elise's heart.

"Mmm-mmm. I knew something smelled mighty good in here." Gray sniffed the air as he lifted Cory up and settled him where he could wrap his legs around Grayson's waist. He carried him past Elise to the breadth of windows, bestowing on her an appreciative smile and a wink as he passed by. "Maybe more than one something."

A spark of awareness passed between them.

"I got to skip school," Cory announced jubilantly. "We got our car back and we went to the grocery store. This place has a washer and dryer in a little room next to the kitchen, did you know that? And Billie Jean wants to move in with us."

"Does she, now?"

"Uh-huh. Doesn't she, Mom?"

Elise looked up from where she'd paused to check on the chicken. "She loves the view. Was thrilled that your sister used to work for *Texas Today* and had a place close to what Billie Jean calls 'all the action.'"

Gray smiled. "Even though the layoff from the magazine was a blow, Maddie's happy to trade it all for ranch life with her fiancé and a job at the local paper. Grasslands is a great town. You'd like it. It's like stepping out of a whirlwind into a cocoon of calm. One of those places where people recognize each other on the street."

"That's the kind of place I come from, too. Cory? Wash your hands, please. It's time to eat."

Gray set the child down and directed him to the bathroom,

then joined Elise in the kitchen. He leaned against the counter, eyes suddenly solemn, looking as if he wanted to say something, but not certain if this was the right time and place.

Elise's fingers fumbled a fork and it clattered to the countertop. Was he going to broach the kiss? Admit it meant something to him—or would he confirm it had been a mistake?

Breath coming unevenly under Gray's steady gaze, she gave him a hesitant smile.

Please, God, I'm confused. So scared. Take me baby step by baby step if this is the direction you want me to go.

Gray glanced around to ensure Cory wasn't within earshot. Then he leaned in, his voice low.

Chapter Twelve

"I got a call from my sister Maddie on my way over here. She's pretty upset."

If I ever get my hands on the guy...

Elise gave her head a slight shake, as if coming out of fog. "Upset? About what?"

"The first kook has oozed out of the woodwork. Called the ranch claiming he knows where Dad is and wants to help the family find him. For a fee."

She placed a hand on his arm. "Oh, Grayson, that's terrible."

"It was bound to happen once word got around."

"But how can you be sure he's a kook, that he doesn't know where your father is?"

"You can't." He'd seen similar situations too many times in law enforcement. "That's what turns a missing person's heartbreak into a potential nightmare."

"So what happens now?"

"I got Maddie calmed down. Called Sheriff Cole and filled him in. He'll get details from my sister and take it from there."

Elise gazed up at him with hope-filled eyes. "Can they trace the call if he phones again?"

"It's not as easily done as what you see on TV." How he wished it were. "The likelihood that guy will call back is slim. Probably a malicious prankster, not a genuine extortionist."

"Either way, that's sick."

"Sad to say, there are a lot of people who get their kicks out of doing things like that."

"I'm so sorry, Grayson."

He hated dumping all this on her, but, just like the other night, it felt good to have someone to share it with. Not just chasing it endlessly around in his own head.

"I'm sorry, too—that I had to spoil your meal tonight with this kind of news. But if Maddie or the sheriff call while I'm here, I'll need to take it. I wanted you to know why."

"Of course. I understand."

He continued to gaze down at her, suddenly remembering last night. How her arms had slipped around his neck… the soft sweetness of her lips on his… "You look mighty pretty tonight."

"Thank you." She dropped her gaze to turn back to the supper preparations and he couldn't help but smile, knowing his words put that soft pink in her cheeks.

She opened a cabinet and pointed at a serving dish on the top shelf. "You're worried about your dad, aren't you?"

"Yeah." He retrieved the dish for her. "We should have heard something by now. Found evidence of his whereabouts."

"You said earlier it isn't uncommon for him to be out of contact, though. That he's devoted to his work."

"Or running from life."

She glanced at him as she rummaged in a drawer. "Why do you say that?"

"Think about it. I've told you a bit about the family situation. How we discovered our dad and mom had been married, had kids, then divorced. Split the two sets of twins and went off to live separate lives. What we don't know is why."

"Sometimes things don't work out."

"There's more to it. It's complicated." But he wasn't ready to share about the paternity issue yet.

She lifted the lid of the electric skillet and set it aside, a mouthwatering, lemony chicken aroma filling the air. Then she turned to him, certainty in her eyes. "You suspect he may have disappeared intentionally and that's why you can't find him."

This woman read him like the proverbial book. "It's crossed my mind."

"But he's a well-respected citizen. A doctor."

"Even well-respected citizens pull up roots and do their best to disappear. If not permanently, at least for a time."

Pausing over the simmering entrée, fork in hand, her gaze appraised him. "Does your family agree with that theory?"

"I haven't discussed it with them, but I wouldn't be surprised if it's the elephant in the room nobody's willing to talk about. Or maybe it's a cop's naturally suspicious nature. But I've come to two conclusions—neither a pretty picture."

"That he's disappeared on purpose—or that he's…dead."

He nodded at her blunt assessment. "What other alternative is there?"

"He could be so busy with doctoring that it hasn't dawned on him anyone is looking for him. Or maybe, like you'd heard, he isn't well. Not bad enough to be hospitalized, but being nursed back to health in someone's home."

"Maybe."

He held the rimmed dish as she transferred the plump chicken pieces to it, then scooped spoonfuls of the rice and fragrant sauce over them.

"You're carrying a heavy load, Grayson. Don't make it heavier than it has to be by dwelling on the negative. I wish there was something I could do to help."

He gave her a rueful smile. "Listening to me rattle on is help enough, reminding me that there's always hope."

"There is. Always."

Much to his disgust, he *had* grown more pessimistic than he used to be. Probably came with the cop territory. Always seeing people at their worst. "I'm concerned about Dad and his whereabouts, but in all honesty, I'm angry with him. I know I shouldn't be but…"

"That's understandable. All these years he's kept your biological mother a secret."

He'd always known his father sometimes seemed troubled. Sad. It didn't go unnoticed that he went to great effort not to let it show for the kids' sake. Grayson always put it down to the loss of his wife, the woman Grayson thought was his birth mother. But there had been so much more….

"Although we loved Rachel like one of the family, Elise, our mother figure was a *nanny*." He shook his head as if in disbelief and lowered his voice further, aware that Cory was elsewhere in the apartment. "Dad could have respected me enough to tell me when I turned eighteen. Now it might be too late to get to know the mother Jack and Violet have always known. What kind of man would withhold that from a child he professed to love?"

And why was *he* dumping all this on Elise?

"He sounds like a confused and hurting man." Her words came softly, the expression in her eyes tender. "But…you're also angry with your…with Belle, aren't you?"

He gave a bitter laugh at how quickly she zeroed in on that. "It sounds silly for a grown man to feel this way. But it's kind of like a kid wandering off at the mall and his mom not coming back for him. I mean, you should hear how Jack and Violet go on about her. That she was such a great mom."

He squared his shoulders, determined to stop sounding like a whiner. What had gotten into him?

"I'm sorry." She lightly touched his arm. "I know it's hard

to understand. And it hurts. But you're going to get your answers, Grayson. It's all going to work out. You have to believe that."

If only he could. But she didn't know the worst of it yet. That Dad might not be his biological father.

He stared down at the dish in his hands, still held in a death grip. Then he gave her a sheepish look. "At the risk of sounding negative, I think supper's getting cold."

"That's what microwaves are for." She smiled, standing on her tippy toes to kiss his cheek as she relieved him of the serving dish. A sweet blush stained her cheeks.

He smiled back, a comforting warmth surging through him as a glimmer of hope flickered somewhere in the recesses of his heart.

Elise.

Surely God hadn't brought her into his life only to let her abandon him, too.

Once seated in front of the windows where last night Grayson had thoroughly kissed her, Elise nodded to Cory to lead the prayer. Eager to eat, he made embarrassingly short work of it. Despite a less than promising start to the evening, Grayson rallied to regale them with stories of his boyhood, omitting any of the anguish she knew his life had held. But his hauntingly sad situation involving his father and birth mother lingered in her mind.

God, please bring some good from all this bad.

When they'd cleaned up after the meal, she sent Cory off to bed early, reminding him that tomorrow would be a school day. He'd have to get up earlier in the morning for the longer drive. To her surprise, Grayson volunteered to tuck him in.

He soon joined her in the living room, sinking into one of the armchairs. From the smile that sent her insides dancing, she sensed the tension from their earlier conversation had eased. Was he now thinking about how they'd held each other last night? Would he say anything about it at all or continue the discussion about his family situation?

"You've got a good kid there, Elise."

"Thank you." She snuggled into the cushioned love seat, thankful that he hadn't gotten a call from Grasslands after all, that they'd have time this evening to talk. "You seem to have a real rapport with little boys."

His eyes twinkled. "Used to be one myself."

"True. But all men were boys once, yet don't always form a bond with children, especially those that aren't their own."

"It's risky."

"Risky?" She laughed. "How do you mean?"

He shrugged. "So it's back to work and school tomorrow?"

"Yes. I dropped off Cory's homework today and picked up what he needed to have done for tomorrow. He's decided living in a high-rise and being homeschooled is the life for him. But I suspect he'd quickly tire of me and miss his friends."

"It's an adventure now."

"Totally." She motioned to the apartment's upscale interior. "I can't thank you enough, Grayson, for arranging a safe haven for us to come to."

"Thank my sister, it's her place."

"But it was your doing. I don't know how I'll ever repay you."

He sank farther back in the chair, looking quite at home. "I don't need to be repaid. But if I was of that inclination, I'd say that incredible meal tonight evened the score."

"I assure you, we won't take advantage of your sister's generosity indefinitely. I'll begin looking at other properties as soon as possible. Strategize how I can move forward on my degree."

"This place is available until the end of the year, so take advantage of it. I don't want you and Cory moving back into that apartment."

She didn't either—if she could help it.

"I also want to apologize for the way I behaved toward you Friday night. For the way I dismissed you as if you'd served your purpose once the source of Cory's misbehavior was brought to light."

He dipped his head slightly in acceptance. "You were upset. I'd forced you to relive that encounter with street hooligans and pushed you about a situation you weren't ready to discuss."

She ran a finger along the upholstery's soft surface. "I'd never told anyone about Duke. I know now I desperately needed to talk to someone about it, but explaining the situation felt as if I was betraying him. I panicked."

"I understand."

All day she'd planned to ask him if he'd be willing to again spend time with Cory. But he'd mentioned something tonight that brought her up short, made her think that he might not want to.

"A few minutes ago, you said forming a bond with little kids is risky. What did you mean by that?"

The startled light in his eyes confirmed she'd caught him off guard with her question.

"Come on now, you already know it's risky to let Cory get attached to someone who's not a family member. My single friends with youngsters are super cautious about that."

"It's only natural." She tucked a strand of hair behind her ear. "You don't want someone waltzing into your life and the life of your child only to waltz back out again. Kids don't understand that behavior. They take it personally. It's instinctive to want to protect them."

"Which is exactly why I say it's risky."

"But that's not solely what you were referring to earlier, was it?"

Gray tensed. "No…I guess not."

"A child isn't the only one who's at risk of getting hurt."

He met her gaze evenly. "No. If a strong bond develops,

it can rip a guy's heart out when the mother decides he's not her cup of tea after all."

"That's happened to you."

"Once."

He rose from the chair to look out at the surrounding skyscrapers, their windows aglow. Who had done that to him and how long ago?

"It was my own fault," he said at last as he turned toward her and shoved his hands into his pants pockets. "I let myself get attached to a girlfriend's four-year-old son. I should have known better."

So that's how he knew about things near and dear to a little boy's heart.

"She'd been antsy from the beginning about my job," he continued, his tone impersonal as if he could divorce himself from the lingering emotion of it. "About the fact I carried a gun. I should have seen it coming, but I didn't. When I told her early last summer that I'd be heading into several months of an undercover assignment she didn't bat an eye. Just showed me the door."

Pain etched his eyes, and her heart ached as she recognized how much it must have cost him to agree to spend time with Cory. "I'm sorry."

"What hurts most is I keep wondering if her son believes I walked off and abandoned him like his father did."

And like Grayson's birth mother had?

"She didn't let you say goodbye? Try to explain?"

"Nope." His gaze drifted again to the window where their reflections mingled with the darkening sky. "It's not the way I'd have handled it if it had been up to me, but our splitting was for the best. She probably saw it long before I did, but I later realized we'd come to think of ourselves as a family unit—not so much because of our relationship with each other, but because of our mutual connection to Michael. Her leaving wasn't the blow I'd expected. But I miss the kid. A lot."

Elise clasped her hands tightly. Grayson was telling her something here.

Something important.

But was he explaining why he didn't intend to get any closer to her? That the kiss had been a mistake never to be repeated? Or was he laying it on her doorstep that if he or Cory got hurt because of a relationship gone bad it would be all her doing?

Well, he'd done it.

Not only spilled his guts last night about how poor pitiful little him hadn't been wanted by his own mother, but how a girlfriend with a kid had dumped him and he'd gotten his feelings hurt. Elise had gone all quiet after that, and the conversation pretty much ground to a halt. Got all awkward. He hadn't stayed long after that.

Now standing outside Maddie's apartment door Thursday evening, awaiting a response to his knock, it dawned on him that maybe she'd expected him to say something about the kiss. He'd thought about it plenty. Too much, in fact. Wondered what Reggie would say about it, too...but wasn't sure he wanted to know. All caught up in the aftermath of Maddie's upset over the malicious caller and memories of Jenna's departure with Michael, he'd gotten sidetracked last night and hadn't said a word about the kiss.

Good going, Wallace.

He glanced impatiently at his watch. Almost eight. She should be home by now. Supper over.

Elise could have brought up the kiss herself, if she'd wanted to, though, right? After all, she'd been the one to initiate it. Sort of. Was she just waiting for him to mention it—or could she be taking his stupid advice and planning to return to Arizona? He shook his head in disgust. Man, what kind of moron suggests to the woman he's fallen in—

The ground all but dissolved under his feet.

Had he fallen in love with Elise? In two weeks? Sure, he was attracted to her. Enjoyed her company and had hoped their relationship might move forward once she got beyond the fact he was a cop.

But...love?

He stared down at the folder in his hand. He'd stayed up last night searching the web. Researching physical therapy programs in the Metroplex. Scouting out security-conscious apartment complexes within reasonable driving distance and not too far from elementary schools.

Is that what someone would do for someone they love?

He gripped the folder tighter. He'd come here tonight with a plan. A surprise he wasn't sure Elise would go for, but one he'd hoped she'd be willing to consider.

Maybe God wanted him to think it over again.

He turned away from the door.

Chapter Thirteen

"Grayson?"

Elise stared down the hall at his retreating form, her insides doing a pirouette. What was he doing here?

He turned, then walked toward her, a folder clutched in his hand and an uncertain look in his eyes.

"I'm sorry, Gray, for not getting to the door more quickly. Cory broke a glass and cut his hand. I was getting him bandaged up."

"Is he going to be okay?" His expression reflected the concern in his tone.

"He'll be fine. Not deep enough for stitches. He's all tucked in for the night now."

He held out the folder to her. "I had some time on my hands last night and cruised around on the web. Thought you might be interested in what I found."

Curious, she opened the folder and flipped through the thick stack of pages. Then stared at him in open-mouthed delight. He'd done this for her? "Oh, my goodness. This must have taken hours." Spare hours he didn't have, what with his ongoing search for his father.

He shrugged. "Hope it helps."

"Oh, it will. It will. Thank you so much!"

He took a step back, as if preparing to leave. He couldn't leave, not now. Not after handing her such a meaningful gift.

"Come in, won't you? We can have a cup of coffee from your sister's fancy machine."

She'd given the situation with his last girlfriend and her son a great deal of thought. Despite the uncertainties of any future relationship between her and Gray, she'd still appreciate his continued involvement with Cory. There had been another episode of pushing and shoving on the playground today when the boy from the previous incident made more inflammatory cracks at Duke's expense. Fortunately, the playground supervisor had broken it up before it escalated to a fight. Would Gray be willing to move on from past disappointments involving a child?

For a moment, she thought he'd decline the invitation. But then he nodded and joined her at the kitchen table while the coffeemaker worked its magic.

"Look at all this. I'm amazed." She eagerly fanned the folder's contents across the table, pausing to scan a page of physical therapy degree requirements. A class schedule for next semester. Gray had suggested she return home, but would a man who wanted you to leave the state go to all this trouble?

He returned her smile, but did he have any idea how seeing all this in front of her made a dream seem more of a possibility? "Oh, Grayson, thank you."

"So how long would it take you to get the degree if you didn't have to work full-time?"

Enthusiasm faded at his words, and she set the pages aside. She'd be lucky to finish in a decade at the rate of one or two courses a semester—if she could afford tuition at all. "There's no point in indulging in that fantasy. It's not an option."

"It could be." His smile quirked as he watched her closely. "How?"

"Scholarships. They have them for women returning to the

workforce. Displaced homemaker grants. Things like that." He tapped the papers. "I put information in here on that, too."

"Thank you, but…" After all the trouble he'd gone through on her behalf, she didn't want to come across as negative. "Maybe a scholarship would cover tuition and books, but the catch is the living expenses."

He looped his good arm over the back of his chair, a satisfied smile playing on his lips. "There are ways to address that, too."

He was full of surprises tonight. She didn't know quite what to make of it.

"I do declare, Officer Wallace." She put a lighthearted lilt into her words. "An officer of the law isn't suggesting I rob a bank is he?"

He grinned. "Noooo. But…what if I help?"

Her smiled faltered. "How do you mean?"

"I'll loan you the money, interest-free, to get yourself and Cory a little apartment not far from the school you pick."

"I can't let you do that."

He leaned forward, his eyes gleaming. "Why not? You think my money is drawing any interest at the bank in this economy? It's sitting there accumulating dust. If I loaned some of it to you, at least it would get a little exercise."

For a moment she held her breath as visions of sailing through her coursework unencumbered by the pressures of a job lit up the too-long darkened corners of her mind. Grayson was serious. He wanted to do this for her. But…how could she possibly let him?

Couldn't he see that allowing him, an almost-stranger, to loan her money would only make her feel she hadn't earned her own way? He'd already done so much for her. But was it out of a sense of duty—or something much more? Something that, in spite of the way she was coming to feel for him, scared her to death.

"I don't know, Grayson. I'm overwhelmed. I—I mean, you hardly know me."

He reached for her hand. "I want to do this for you, Elise. For you and Cory."

She stared at him, marveling at his generosity yet, true to her nature, questioning his motives. "I can't accept—"

"No strings attached," he hurried on, rightly interpreting one of the reasons for her reluctance. "No obligations. Strictly business."

"I don't know what to say, Grayson. I just know I can't—"

"You don't need to decide tonight. Take your time. Think it over."

"I will." But she wouldn't. She'd already made up her mind, but didn't want to argue with him. "Thank you."

Shaken, she rose to get their coffee, certain she'd hurt his feelings for not immediately accepting. He'd obviously gone out of his way to help her, anticipating that she'd be overjoyed at the prospect of finally realizing her dream. But instead, she'd all but ungratefully refused.

When she turned to the table once again, she noticed he'd gathered the thick stack of papers and returned them to the folder. She handed him a mug, but remained standing. "Cory had a little skirmish today."

Gray frowned, no doubt taking notice of the abrupt change in topic. "What set this one off?"

"Same kid as last time. Slurs on Duke."

His mouth took a downward turn, but she rushed on. "I know it's a lot to ask after what you shared last night about your former girlfriend and her boy, but—"

A shoulder lifted, dismissing her comment. "I probably made it sound worse than it was."

She tightened the grip on her mug. "I suspect the opposite. Which is why I'm hesitant to ask this."

"Ask away."

"I'd told you that once I learned the source of Cory's behavioral issues, I'd handle matters on my own. But I think I spoke too soon."

He lifted a brow. "You want me to spend more one-on-one time with him?"

"I understand if you're reluctant to do that. But I thought maybe you could take Cory on an outing on Sunday, that is, if you don't have family business to attend to in Grasslands this weekend." Goodness only knew, he had enough to deal with on that front. "Maybe to the zoo? It would give the two of you time to talk before school rolls around again on Monday."

Something that looked unmistakably akin to guilt flickered in his eyes, and the muscles in Elise's stomach tightened.

"*This* Sunday afternoon?"

She nodded. "After church and lunch. I thought it might be a nice surprise for him. Something to look forward to."

"Sure wish I could but, um…" He glanced away, almost as if not wanting to look her in the eye. "I have a…prior commitment."

An invisible fist punched her in the stomach. *Duke.* How often had she heard his excuses, his "prior commitments" and never had a clue what was really going on?

Can't today, 'lise, have to help Sam with his boat.

Sorry, sweetheart, something's come up.

I forgot to tell you, but I promised to watch the game at Ken's.

"That's okay." Shaken by the intensity of the memory, she nevertheless managed to force a smile as she studied Grayson's still-averted face as he gazed into his coffee mug. "It was just a thought. Even though there were some problems today, Cory's putting extra effort into school. He got a good grade on his math test. I thought some time with you…"

"I'm more than happy to spend a few hours with Cory. Just not…Sunday." Still looking uncomfortable, he downed his coffee and stood. "Why don't I touch base with you in a few days and we can compare schedules?"

"Okay. Thanks."

They chatted a few more minutes about inconsequential things. When he'd headed on his way, she set the locks, then leaned back against the door. It was so unlike Gray to behave like that. Guilty. Nervous.

What was he hiding?

"You didn't invite her, did you?"

Gray looked up from his desk to meet his friend's accusing eye. "Look, Reggie, like I said before, an afternoon of football with the gang is premature."

"Cops hang out with cops."

"So? Elise and I aren't that far into a relationship."

"Not too far is when you need to talk about it. If you can't talk openly with her now, you're asking for trouble."

Gray's mind flickered to the night he'd told Elise about his family. His frustrations. He'd talked things out and she'd listened. But discussing police work and surrounding her with cops? Not yet. He had a lot of thinking to do. Was it right to put Elise to the test before he'd even passed it himself?

"You worry too much, Reg. Things are under control."

"Right." His pal waved him off and headed down the hall.

Gray tossed his pen to the desktop. Maybe Reggie was right. He should have at least told her what he was doing on Sunday. But he wanted to buy some time, decide where he wanted to go with his career. Then he'd be free to figure out a way to get her to go along with him in whatever direction that might be.

It had been dumb, though, to offer her a loan. Jumping the gun. He could see it on her face the second the words were out of his mouth. In chatting with his physical therapist, he'd learned how she'd gotten sufficient credits under her belt to start as a physical therapy assistant as she worked toward a full degree and then a master's. While it would be challenging, especially with a little kid in tow, it sounded doable. He'd thought it might raise Elise's spirits to know it could happen more quickly than she believed.

But that chin of hers had lifted ever so slightly, and he knew her pride had gotten in the way. Again. Either that or she thought he was manipulating her. Trying to make her feel obligated to him. But he wasn't. He just wanted her—and Cory—to have a better life.

But he should have held off and waited to see where the relationship went. Kept his mouth shut. Maybe Reggie was right. He needed to back off before one or both of them got hurt.

"Something's bothering you." Billie Jean probed over the phone late Saturday morning, shortly after Elise and Cory returned from grocery shopping. "What's up?"

"This probably sounds silly." She lowered her voice and slipped into the bedroom where Cory wouldn't hear. Gently closed the door. "But I get the feeling Grayson's hiding something."

"He isn't Duke, Elise."

She'd finally told Billie Jean the whole story of what had brought her and Cory to Fort Worth, so now she had another friend to confide in. "I know that."

"Don't go paranoid here, honey. Most men don't harbor anything darker than agreeing to a diet and indulging in a cheeseburger and fries when out from under the watchful eyes of their spouse."

"It's just that Thursday night when I asked him if he'd take Cory to the zoo on Sunday, he said he had a previous engagement—and looked so guilty about it."

And not just guilty, but sentenced and serving time.

"Is it unreasonable that he might have a life apart from

you and your kid? You keep forgetting you've only known him a couple of weeks."

Two weeks? Impossible. It seemed like forever.

"I told you it sounds silly, but something furtive flashed through his eyes. Secretive. Like whatever he was doing he didn't want me to know about."

"You mean like a date?"

Billie Jean's words jolted. Could he have kissed her like he did and already be off with another woman? No, that wasn't the Gray she'd come to know. From the look on his face that night, it was clear he'd thought whatever he was up to would bring him down in her estimation. Something that would make her regret the kiss—and that she'd allowed him into Cory's life.

"I get the impression the guy is squeaky clean, hon. As honest as the day is long." That's what everyone had thought about Duke, too. "So, when will you see him again?"

"I don't know. He said he'd get in touch with me. I need to look for a new place, anyway. At least a temporary one. I can't stay here indefinitely."

"I don't know why you're in such an all-fired hurry to get out of there. I mean, he's helping you break the lease on the place over here so you can save your rent money."

"Can't you see, though? I'm falling into the same pattern I did with Duke. 'The man' doing everything while I sit passively by and let him." She tightened her grip on the phone. "Look where a history of that landed me. I've had to grow up these past two years and I sense myself sliding back into that old comfort zone. Letting a man control things."

"I don't think Cory's cop is trying to control things, Elise. I think he cares for you and wants to help."

"In case you haven't noticed, Grayson has a major rescuer complex. You know, a save-the-day mentality."

"Comes in handy when you're a cop," Billie Jean quipped.

"Maybe so, but it's out of place in a romantic relationship."

"Come again?"

"It's kind of like I'm one of many he rides to the rescue for. The food bank. Friends and neighbors. Always stepping in to lend a helping hand. Superhero. I don't want to be some man's charity case."

Billie Jean's laugh almost turned into a howl. "A charity case? Honey, believe me, a charity case isn't what that man sees when he takes a look at you."

"Still, it's not right to take advantage of him. And I have my pride."

"Won't argue with that."

Elise narrowed her eyes. "What's that supposed to mean?"

"If it wasn't for that pride of yours, you wouldn't be living in Fort Worth right now barely scratching by. You'd be living with your folks until you get yourself back on your feet. But no, you have to keep up the pretense that Duke was without faults and that you don't need anyone else."

"Of course I need other people. I appreciate all you've done for me. I hope someday to make it up to you. I owe you so much."

"Being appreciative is one thing. Thinking you owe me anything for being a friend is that pride of yours again." Billie Jean sighed. "Look, I gotta start lunch for Roy and the boys. Talk to you later."

Grayson had spoken of her pride, too. What is it he'd said? Something along the lines of not letting it prevent her from going home where she belonged.

But pride was a good thing, wasn't it? Not the haughty, pompous type, but the kind that was evidence of self-respect, a mark of personal dignity. Weren't people always saying "you should be proud of yourself" or "take pride in your work"? Why, then, was *her* pride a target to be shot down?

Well, pride or no pride, she didn't intend to stay in his sister's apartment if Grayson was seeing someone else—or up to something of a darker nature.

Already a plan was formulating. She'd get to the bottom of that guilty look and make him come clean.

Chapter Fourteen

This was a bad idea.

Elise drove through the attractive, well-established neighborhood of two-story townhouses. Full-grown trees. Curbside flower pots. Like most residential areas featuring condos and apartments, there were quite a few cars parked along the length of the quiet street.

The muscles in her upper arms tightened. Grayson's SUV in the driveway confirmed the number he'd scrawled on the back of the business card he'd given Cory. So what was the "prior commitment"?

"Is this Officer Grayson's house, Mom?" Cory started to unbuckle his seatbelt.

"Hang on. I need to find a place to park." She needed a few minutes to get her head cleared, too. Calm her breathing. For the millionth time since she'd set out, she asked herself what she hoped to gain from this. But the more she thought about his reaction to her request to spend time with Cory, the more she was sure he was hiding something.

A few minutes later, she snagged a plastic-wrapped plate from the backseat. Homemade cookies to give her an excuse for showing up. With Cory at her side, she approached a small covered porch, noting the rocked yard and neatly trimmed bushes. Potted petunias on the doorstep.

Before she could stop him, Cory ran up and repeatedly rang the doorbell. To her relief, even after a full minute, Grayson hadn't come to the door. Maybe he wasn't home after all, but had gone off with someone. She could leave the cookies on his doorstep and slip away. Or take them with her, leaving him none the wiser as to her ill-thought-out visit.

"It doesn't look like—"

The air sucked out of Elise's lungs as the door opened. An attractive blonde in a Dallas Cowboys T-shirt and capris swept a curious gaze over them. Oh. No. It *was* a date.

"Chocolate chips!" The woman gave a squeal and placed her hand to her heart as if in a swoon. Then she held open the screen door. "You sweet things. Come on in, y'all."

A wave of heat flooded through Elise as she placed a hand on Cory's shoulder to keep him from darting through the open door.

"What's this about chocolate chips?" a familiar male voice rumbled and she wished herself on another planet. Or at least as far as Austin.

Before she could catch her breath, Grayson appeared behind the woman. For a blinding moment his gaze locked with Elise's, his dismay more than evident.

The blonde looked up at him, accusation glinting in her eyes. If ever a man looked guilty, this one did, which made her feel even worse about showing up on his doorstep.

"Officer Grayson! We brought you cookies."

"Hey there, Cory. This is a surprise. Come on in."

Elise took a step back. "No, no, we—"

But Cory had already squeezed between Grayson and the woman and into the house.

"Cory! I'm sorry. I— Cory and I baked cookies after church, and we thought you might like some." She held them out as if presenting a peace offering, hoping her expression conveyed to Grayson her regret for invading his personal space.

"I'll take custody of those if you don't mind." The woman reached for the plate. "Get yourself on in here, honey."

Grayson, appearing uncomfortable, motioned toward the home's interior. "Yeah, come on in. Bearers of cookies are always welcome."

She'd retrieve Cory and make her escape.

Gray ushered her into the adjoining living room before closing the door behind her. Trapped.

From the back of the condo, the voice of a television sports announcer reached her ears. Cory had apparently already disappeared in that direction.

"Your manners are atrocious, Gray." The woman jabbed him none too gently in the ribs with her elbow, then turned to Elise with an exasperated look as if to say "men!"

"Hi, I'm Pam Cavert."

"Elise Lopez."

"Good to meet you. How do you know Gray?"

Direct and to the point. "He met my son when speaking at a school career day and, um—" She didn't want to tell this stranger Cory had behavior problems and he'd come to the rescue. Or that she and Gray had gotten, well, kissing-close.

"Cory and I hit it off," Grayson clarified, looking to Elise for confirmation. "I signed on to mentor him."

"Oh, really?" Pam's eyes narrowed with a speculative gleam, one now tinged with more amusement than Elise would have felt if a strange woman had shown up on *her* boyfriend's doorstep, claiming a connection he'd told her nothing about. "I didn't know you were into helping guide little kids."

"Which shows you, Pam, you don't know as much about me as you think you do." He folded his arms, a smug smile tugging his lips. "Pam is a police officer in my division.

Prides herself on her intuition and observational skills. Looks like she fell short this time."

A roar of shouts from the back of the house startled Elise and she looked to the pair in alarm.

Pam laughed, waving for Elise to follow. "Cowboys must have scored against the Arizona Cardinals. Come meet the gang."

The gang?

Elise glanced at a sheepish-looking Grayson, but he merely motioned for her to precede him.

When they entered a family room at the rear of the house—a massive widescreen TV its dominant decorative feature—she halted, her mouth going desert dry. Pam waded into a sea of men and women to set the cookies on a coffee table amidst chips, dips, popcorn and a tray of sub sandwiches.

And there was Cory smack in the middle of the room, a sandwich in his hand.

"Half time, babe!" a stocky, dark-haired man reported to Pam as he stood to stretch. Then he snatched up a chocolate chip cookie. "Cowboys twelve, Cards six."

Pam fist-punched the air, then clapped her hands for attention. "Hey, y'all. You've met Cory. This is his mom, Elise Lopez. Looks like Grayson here's been holding out on us."

A roomful of curious faces turned toward Elise. A few women clapped. One guy wolf-whistled. There must have been over a dozen guests, mostly males, crammed into the space. She took a step back and bumped into Grayson who steadied her, apparently aware of the impact the fit, clean-cut crew had on her.

"So he's not taken a vow of celibacy after all," one big guy joked, wiping his brow as if in relief. Others quickly joined in with their own good-natured wisecracks.

"I don't know where Gray found ya, sweetheart, but I'd say you're worth the wait."

"You sure you want to hang out with this bozo? I could tell you a few stories…"

"Hey, Pam, how'd Gray slip this past you?"

With a laugh, Pam quickly pointed out the people in the room, giving them names Elise knew she'd never remember.

She was too numb.

The roaring in her ears too loud.

From the moment she'd stepped across the threshold, she knew without a doubt she'd come upon her personal equivalent of a viper pit.

A den of cops.

It was clear she'd stayed only because of Cory.

Warmly embraced by Grayson's friends, the boy's face glowed when he'd realized most present were police officers.

Now, having followed the pair back to his sister's place, ensuring they safely reached their destination in the dark, Gray kicked himself for not telling her about the football gathering. Sure, she'd have turned down his invitation, but at least she wouldn't have been thrown into their midst unprepared. How was he to know, though, that she'd show up on his doorstep?

Naturally, his pals assumed she was his special lady. With one look at the beautiful Elise, no one would have bought a "just friends" denial, so he hadn't tried to correct their misconception.

Come to think of it, she hadn't, either.

"Elise?"

He turned to her as Cory dashed out the high-rise's elevator door and down the hall leading to the apartment. Her eyes met his in silent question.

"Thanks for the cookies."

A faint smile brightened her features. "Did you even get any? I don't know when I've seen so many human vacuums with such capacity."

"I managed to snag one. Good, too." He raked a hand through his hair. "I, uh, I'm sorry I didn't tell you about the cop thing. I know it was uncomfortable for you."

She stepped out of the elevator and he joined her. "Duke often packed our place with a bunch of football fanatics. It brought back memories."

"I'm sorry."

"Don't be. Cory loved it. Everyone was so nice when he announced he was the son of Duke Lopez."

"Yeah, they're a great bunch."

Side by side, they started down the hall.

"I'm going to put Cory straight to bed. School night. Would you like to come in? Say good-night to him?"

She probably thought he owed her that much, with Cory practically bouncing off the walls with excitement after hours in the midst of Gray's law-enforcement friends. Helping get him calmed down was the least he could do.

"Sure."

Once inside he lingered in the living room, listening to Cory's enthusiastic tones and Elise's quiet murmurings as she prepared him for bed. A quick bath. Teeth brushing.

"Officer Grayson?" Cory appeared at his side, smelling of bath soap and toothpaste. The little guy hiked up the waistband of his baggy pajama bottoms as Gray crouched next to him.

"Yeah, bud?"

Cory's smile stretched wide. "You have cool friends."

"Yeah, I do."

"They even know who my dad is. That he's a hero."

"Policemen are like that, Cory. Kind of like family."

The boy leaned into him for an unexpected hug, then drew back, his eyes solemn. "Can I come to your house again? I'll tell Mom to bring cookies."

Gray stood and carefully lifted him into his arms. How should he answer that? If he said no, what reason would he give that wouldn't be interpreted as rejection? But if he said yes, wasn't that making a promise he might not keep? Too often he regretted things he'd told Jenna's Michael. *Sure, I'll teach you how to do that. Let's hit that Disney movie when it comes to town. When you're a little older, we'll take in a Cowboys game.*

Promises casually made. All of them broken.

Did Michael remember them? Think he was a liar?

Cory patted his slinged shoulder. "So can I?"

"We'll see. I'm not home much."

"That's because you're at my house a lot."

He chuckled. "You think so?"

"Yeah. You like us."

The honest observation pierced his heart. "Yeah, I do."

Smiling, the boy rested his head against Gray's shoulder. "Getting sleepy?"

Cory nodded, his soft hair brushing Gray's neck.

"Then let's get you tucked into bed." He turned in the direction of the bedroom and paused. Elise stood but a dozen feet away, quietly watching them, her gaze troubled.

If only he could kiss away that expression as easily as he had put Cory's concerns to rest.

Despite the day's excitement, he hadn't gotten far into reading a dog story aloud before the boy's brown eyes fluttered closed. Rhythmic breathing followed and, as Gray stared down at him, a tenderness that was almost painful knifed his heart.

Duke Lopez had been one lucky guy.

Or maybe not.

He tucked the covers around Cory's small frame, then turned off the bedside lamp. Shut the door. Entering the living room, he snagged his jacket from the back of a chair. "Guess I'd better get going."

"Thank you for seeing us home."

"My pleasure." He moved to stand before her, drinking in her beauty. The still-troubled expression.

She took an uncertain breath. "I have a confession to make, Grayson."

He quirked a smile. "Do I need to read you your rights? Get you legal counsel?"

She smiled at his attempt to lighten the mood. "No, but I want to apologize for crashing your party. I know you were surprised to see Cory and me."

"I have to admit I wasn't expecting a cookie delivery."

"It was…more than a cookie delivery. I was checking up on you."

He cocked an eyebrow. "Checking up on me?"

"I was determined to find out what your 'prior commitment' was that prevented you from taking Cory to the zoo." She hung her head. "It's not a pretty thing to admit, but I have a suspicious nature. I didn't used to, but—"

He tilted her head to look at him as truth dawned. "You thought I was up to something I didn't want you to know about. Like Duke."

"I'm sorry. I feel so foolish."

He placed a finger to her soft lips. "Say no more."

"But I have to. I wish I wasn't like this. After all you've done for Cory and me, not trusting you is inexcusable. I'll understand if you feel it best not to involve yourself further with either of us."

Could he do that? Walk away from Cory? From her? Being with Elise felt right. More right than any other relationship he'd experienced in his entire life. When they were together, did she not sense the connection as he did?

"Are you trying to find a nice way of saying you want me to move on?" He gazed into her anxious eyes, hoping she saw in his the wishes of his heart. "I can't move on. And I won't."

He slipped his unfettered arm around her waist and drew a startled Elise close. "Stupid sling. A man has the opportunity to get his arms around a beautiful woman and it thwarts him at every turn."

For a moment she held herself rigid, staring into his eyes. Then her lips curved ever so slightly as she relaxed into him, welcoming a repeat performance of Tuesday night's sweet interlude.

When the kisses came to a reluctant end, he gently brushed the hair back from her face. "I'm coming to care for you very much, Elise. If I'm not mistaken, you have feelings for me, too. Don't you think it's time we stopped pretending otherwise?"

"Gray, I—"

"We both have a ton of baggage we're toting around. A lot of challenges to get beyond. So where do we go from here?"

Chapter Fifteen

"I'm not sure," she whispered, "that we can go anywhere."

Under the palms of her hands she felt his chest swell as he took a labored breath. "I'm here to stay if you'll have me, Elise. I'm here for both you and Cory. For the long haul."

"That's what Duke thought, too. But it wasn't his decision to make. A man with a gun made it for him."

Gray's eyes gentled. "What happened to him is rare. Extremely rare."

"You say that, but you can't be unaware that scores of officers in this country died in the line of duty last year. That's not rare, Grayson, no matter how you look at it."

"But the statistical odds…"

She pulled back. "Don't quote a gambler's mantra to me, Grayson. I can't play the odds with Cory's life."

"Cory's life? Or your own?"

She sighed softly, searching for the words to explain. Words that wouldn't hurt him but would make it clear that loving her might not be in his best interests.

"I had no idea when I married Duke," she murmured, "how every moment, whether waking or sleeping, I'd be on guard. Alert. Keeping an ear tuned to the news. Dreading a phone call late at night when he was on duty."

"I know it had to be hard."

Her lips formed a trembling smile. "And, oh, how I'd cling to him each time he walked through the door."

Gray caught her hand in his. Gave it a reassuring squeeze. "A friend tells me it takes a special woman to be the wife of a police officer."

"I'm not worthy of that kind of admiration."

"Elise—"

"No, listen to me." She tightened her grip on his hand. "The night...the night Duke was killed, Cory was at a sleepover with a friend from church. I knew Duke would be late, so planned supper for nine. But then he didn't come. Not ten. Not eleven."

His thumb caressed her hand as she relived those hours. Extinguishing candles. Refrigerating the meal. Prayerfully moving around the darkened house. Watching the clock.

"Shortly after midnight the doorbell rang. Two officers—" She blinked back tears. "They took me to the hospital. But—" Choking on a sob every bit as painful as any from two years ago, she squeezed Gray's strong hand. "He was gone before I arrived. He never knew I was there."

"I'm sorry, Elise."

"So don't you see?" She stared into his eyes. "I can't go through that again. I can't lose you, too."

He drew her to him, murmuring soothing words against her hair. She closed her eyes and burrowed into him, shutting out the too-vivid memories of that night. The hospital sounds and smells. The hushed voices. Would she never stop thinking of it? Dreaming about it?

"I understand. I won't rush you. Won't pressure. I know I'm asking a lot of you to give yourself to another lawman." He drew back to cup her face in his hand, his eyes tender. "But with all my heart I believe God has a good plan for us. I'll do whatever it takes. Wait as long as you need to work through this. I'll help you in any way I can."

"I can't make any promises, Grayson. Not yet."

Maybe not ever.

"I don't expect you to. But the Good Book says there are seasons in life. A time to weep and a time to laugh. A time to mourn and one in which to dance. You're coming into your time—our time—to laugh and dance, Elise."

The next two days were like a dream. Grayson came by the apartment after work each evening. Ate with them and played with Cory. After tucking her son in for the night, they stayed up for hours talking about their pasts. Their families. Values. Beliefs. Anything that came to mind.

Grayson told her about him and his siblings receiving Bibles and the same puzzling, anonymous notes. About the painful possibility that his dad might not be his biological father. How although he was loath to resort to DNA testing behind his father's back, wouldn't definitive proof of his true paternity explain so much?

She encouraged him to write down his feelings in the form of letters or emails—either to send to his dad once he was found or just to get the confusion and anger out of his system. She then explained how her parents cautioned her not to marry Duke right out of high school. How, concerned that she'd become too dependent on Duke, they'd advised her to complete her education first. But she hadn't listened, which made it all the harder to face them and admit Duke's gambling addiction.

To her amazement, during those Grayson-filled hours of laughter, tears and sharing from the heart, Elise's fears became less pronounced. Not faded away entirely—she wasn't that naive. But it gave her courage that with God's help—and Grayson's support—building a life with another police officer might not be out of the question. She'd never felt safer with anyone in her entire life. She just needed more time to be sure she wasn't promising something to Grayson she couldn't give him.

"I'm going to Grasslands this weekend," Grayson announced over the phone early Wednesday evening. "Didn't you say Cory gets Friday off due to something in the school's schedule? Take the day off, too. Come with me."

She cringed. Cory endlessly begged to see the ranch. "Don't feel obligated to make this happen for him right now."

"It will be fun for all of us. Like I've told you, Grasslands is the best of what small towns have to offer." She could hear the smile in his voice. "Antiques shops, a country-cookin' restaurant, and my sister Violet runs a great produce market. There's lots for kids to do, too. And you'll love the little church."

"It does sound wonderful." How she'd love to escape the city rush. Go for a walk under the stars. "But this is a difficult time for your family. They don't need a stranger and her kid invading their space."

"You won't even be a blip on the radar. Jack, Violet and Maddie will have their significant others there and they're all just getting to know each other. Maddie's soon-to-be stepdaughter will make a perfect playmate for Cory. Come on. I bet the two of us could even find ourselves a private place for a little more kissing."

"Gray!" She laughed at his confident approach to their relationship. But how would he explain their in-limbo situation to his family? Although she was rapidly warming to a future with Grayson, would his family's assumption that something serious was in the works pressure them? "You make it sound so tempting, but I think we'd better wait. Maybe next time."

"I'm leaving first thing Friday morning. Let me know if you change your mind."

True to his promise not to pressure her, he didn't insist they accompany him. Said he'd check in tomorrow. But two seconds after saying goodbye, the phone rang again and she took the call without checking caller ID.

"No, I haven't changed my mind!" she teased, a giggle in her voice.

"And what would you be refusing to change your mind about, hon?" Billie Jean's distinctive drawl brought visions of the too-handsome Grayson to a screeching halt.

She laughed. "Oh. Sorry. I thought you were someone else."

"You didn't turn down a proposal from that good-lookin' Boy Scout of yours, did you?"

"No. Just a weekend at his family's ranch."

"Why'd you turn him down?" From the tone of her friend's voice, she obviously thought that was a stupid move. "He doesn't strike me as the type to bring women home to the family on a casual whim."

"That's just it. If I show up with him, won't his family assume there's something going on between us?"

"Remind me again where the flaw is in that picture?"

"It would be awkward any way you look at it." Billie Jean didn't know the story of Gray's family, and Elise wasn't at liberty to share it with her. "I'm not comfortable with imposing on his family, taking advantage of their hospitality."

"Girl, a romantic weekend in the country with Mr. Law Enforcement is exactly what you need right now. If he hasn't kissed you yet, it would be a grand opportunity to make your move. But he has already—hasn't he?"

"What kind of question is that?"

Billie Jean laughed. "I suspected as much. Thought he seemed like a man of action. I suppose he's a good kisser, too."

"Billie Jean!"

"Figured he would be. Why don't you relax and see where this leads? Why are you always fightin' the good Lord when he's trying to do his best to take care of you?"

Is that what she was doing? Fighting against God—not just Grayson and her fears? But she wasn't up to getting into this tonight with Billie Jean. "I assume you called to do more than get on my case."

"I wanted you to know Roy and I are fixin' to go down to Kaufman County this weekend to visit his cousin. I won't keep you any longer—I imagine you're expecting Grayson any minute."

"Actually, he's doing volunteer work at a men's shelter this evening." He was always thinking of others. Reaching out a helping hand to those in need, even outside police work.

"So what are you doing tonight?"

"I have a paper for an online class to research and need to study for a test. I promised a veggie tray for the office potluck, too. Plus I need to clean up around here. Do laundry."

"You're gonna have to slow down someday, Elise. And when you finally do, you don't want to be looking behind you and seeing all the stuff you missed. Stuff God was standin' there holding out to you but you were too stubborn to accept."

When the call ended, Elise headed to the utility room to start the laundry. *Was* God trying to answer her prayers, trying to fill the lonely hours since Duke's passing? Was He attempting to find her a home and a man she could respect and love—one who would love and respect her, too?

With a silent prayer, she hurried to her phone. Hit a speed dial number. Held her breath.

"Wallace," the familiar voice responded.

"It's me, Elise. About your invitation…"

Grayson's heart pounded with anticipation Thursday evening as he pulled the duffel and clothes bag out of the closet. Elise and Cory would be going to Grasslands with him tomorrow. It would be over five sweet hours in Elise's company. A little longer if they not only stopped for lunch but for coffee or ice cream as well—which he'd make sure they did.

He smiled to himself. He'd talk his sisters into keeping Cory occupied so he could sneak in a stroll around the ranch with Elise. Show her that little house he'd spotted in town. And who knows—maybe they could find an out-of-they-way place to do some snuggling.

He chuckled. Yeah, he was putting all his eggs in one basket with this trip. But getting Elise away from the stresses of her everyday world might work in his favor. It would give her the opportunity to see him interacting with his siblings. Let her see he wasn't "all cop." He could count on Maddie to put in a good word on his behalf. Violet would, too. Maybe even Jack. With the whole gang on his side, how could he go wrong?

His cell phone signaled an incoming call.

"Officer Wallace, this is Deputy Sheriff Nolan Campton."

Gray drew in a breath. The deputy was one of many in South Texas he'd spoken with in recent weeks. "Have you found Brian Wallace?"

"No, sir, I regret to say that we haven't. But someone turned in his wallet yesterday. They'd found it in a ditch somewhere out in the county."

"Somewhere?" That sounded mighty vague.

"A volunteer team was picking up trash on a long, barren stretch of road a week or two ago. One of them found the wallet, but wasn't in town to turn it in until yesterday afternoon."

"Cash and credit cards intact?"

"No cash. But credit cards and IDs."

"The absence of cash doesn't mean he was robbed." He wouldn't let himself dwell on that possibility.

"No, sir. He might not have had any or someone could have found the wallet before the roadside team discovered it. Helped himself to the cash."

"Right. Or his wallet may have been found fifty miles away and tossed out the window of a speeding car once divested of anything deemed valuable. Not everyone's willing to risk credit card fraud or identity theft."

The deputy grunted his agreement. "We did send one of our men out that way. He talked to folks who live in the vicinity, but none had spoken with or seen anyone fitting the description of Brian Wallace."

"The area's sparsely populated, isn't it? A stranger would likely be noticed."

"Correct."

"No sign of his vehicle?"

"No, sir. I'm sorry, but we'll keep you posted."

As he shut off the phone, he sent a plea heavenward. His dad was sick. Possibly extremely sick. Had no cell phone. No cash. No credit cards. No ID.

Why hadn't he at least gotten himself to a phone to call him or Maddie? Asked someone to call for him? Was he that bad off? While nonsinister explanations could be derived for the wallet being found where it was, it didn't bode well for the possible state of his father's mental or physical health.

Or did it confirm Brian Wallace had put the past behind him, determined to slip away to a less-complicated future?

He'd just have to start calling around area hospitals and clinics again. Touch base with those he'd spoken to earlier. Probe deeper. Since his dad didn't have ID with him, that complicated things. But at least no bodies in need of positive identification had been reported. Yet.

He pressed Jack's speed dial number, then cut it off before it rang. No point in delivering the disturbing news over the phone. He'd be there by tomorrow afternoon and could share what he knew then. Looked like the trip wouldn't be quite the romantic respite he'd hoped for. Nevertheless, he'd do his best to see Elise and Cory had a good time.

But where was Brian Wallace?

Chapter Sixteen

"Is this everything?"

Grayson's voice echoed in the shadowed, underground parking of the high-rise apartment building Friday morning.

Elise nodded as he effortlessly lifted what she knew was a too-heavy suitcase to the back of his SUV. They'd only be gone a few days, but she intended to be prepared.

"Yes, that's it."

After rearranging the luggage, he shut the rear hatch. "Then let's get moving. We're burning daylight."

Was it her imagination or was Grayson on edge this morning? He seemed all-business, anxious to get to his family's home. Or was he nervous about bringing her and Cory along? Maybe he was having second thoughts.

He opened the front-passenger-side door for Elise. Then helped Cory into the back and shut the door just as his cell phone rang.

Impatiently checking the caller ID, he stepped a short distance from the vehicle, shooting her an apologetic glance.

"Hey, Cameron. What's up?" A pause. "Yeah, I'm taking the day off. Family business."

Another pause. He laughed. "No foolin'? Glad they're

pleased. Maybe they'll poke a little something extra in my next paycheck."

Elise tried not to eavesdrop, but couldn't help herself with the window rolled down and him standing not a dozen feet from her.

"What? Yeah, that's good news, all right." He chuckled, seemingly pleased. "We made a successful bust that looks like it's headed for a conviction, but sometimes you wonder. Didn't get much more than a pat on the back the time I talked that guy into putting down the gun and letting his girlfriend go. What?"

A long silence ensued as he listened intently to the caller. The light in his eyes dimmed and a guarded gaze flickered in Elise's direction. "No, I hadn't heard that. When did it happen?"

A cold finger traced down her spine as she strained to hear his next words.

"Domestic violence calls are the worst, especially if there's alcohol or drug abuse involved. You never know if the one who placed the call will turn on you. No, that doesn't sound good."

Her throat tightened. A police officer injured.

"How's Sylvia holding up? Man, I hope he pulls through. He told me Sunday afternoon they're trying to start a family."

A wave of nausea roiled through Elise's stomach. One of the men she'd met at Gray's. One of the men who'd been so nice to Cory. *Please, God, please don't let him die. Please.*

"Well, he's a fighter. Keep me posted, will you? Yeah, you, too."

Gray sucked in a ragged breath as he pocketed his phone. He didn't look at her, but came around the front of the SUV, jaw hard as he settled into the driver's seat.

"What happened?"

He met her gaze with a bleak one of his own, then glanced in the rearview mirror at Cory who was listening to a kid's book downloaded to Gray's iPod. He kept his voice low. "Officer responding to a domestic disturbance a few hours ago. Scott. You met him and Sylvia on Sunday."

Her memory flashed to a lanky redhead with a winning sense of humor and a brunette who gazed at him just short of adoration. "It's bad, isn't it?"

He nodded. "Yeah. Real bad."

He adjusted his side mirror, then shoved the key into the ignition.

Her hand stayed him.

"Gray." She could barely choke out the words. "I'm sorry, but it's not a good idea for Cory and me to join you this weekend."

His brows lowered. "Why not?"

"You and me. It's…not going to work." She reached for the door handle with icy fingers. "Hop on out, Cory."

"Now hang on a minute, Elise."

Gray reached for her, but she pulled away. Got out. Slammed the door behind her. He was out his door and by her side before she could get the back door open. He clasped her arm and turned her toward him.

Shaking inside, she stared at him. "I can't go through this. I just can't. Not again."

"We talked about this, remember? Came to an understanding. The seasons thing."

"Your season will always be law enforcement. You should have seen your face when you got the first half of that call that your superiors are pleased with you. You love police work." Couldn't he see the truth? She could never take that away from him. "You'd never be happy doing anything else— and I can never be happy knowing you're on the streets with people who want to kill you."

She motioned toward the SUV and raised her voice. "Come on, Cory, let's go."

"Stay put, Cory," he countermanded.

She frowned when her son obeyed Gray over her. "Would you please get our luggage?"

"Elise—"

"I can't tell you how sorry I am. But please, Grayson, don't fight me on this."

His voice hardened. "You're going to disappoint that little boy. He can hardly wait to see the ranch. If you don't want to come, let me take him."

"By himself?"

"You know he's safe with me. Please don't make it look like I made a promise I'm not keeping."

Why did he have to put her in this position, reminding her of that other little boy who haunted him? "You have family things to attend to. He'd be in the way."

"He wouldn't. But if you won't do it for Cory, do it for me. I didn't want to say anything to spoil the trip, but I could use some moral support myself."

She shook her head, not understanding.

He ran his hand along the back of his neck, frustration evident. "I got a call last night from a deputy sheriff down south."

Oh, please, Lord, not more bad news. "About your dad?"

"They found his wallet, but no sign of him. I want to deliver the news to my family in person. Didn't feel like doing it over the phone last night."

"But don't you think that's all the more reason Cory and I shouldn't go with you?" The tension in her stomach increased. "Your family shouldn't have to attend to the needs of strangers at a time like this."

"Dad's disappearance has weighed on us for weeks. Having Cory around will help keep our minds off this turn of events. Besides, they're expecting you."

"I don't know…"

"We need time to talk, too. Work things out."

She shook her head. Talking wouldn't work out their differences. "Gray, we need to be honest with ourselves. I can't deal with living life edged by fear. Not again."

"We can face your fears together."

"That's not—"

"Just come with me, Elise. For Cory's sake."

He reached for her hand and gently clasped it.

It hadn't been a pleasant drive for the three of them.

Maybe he'd been wrong to pressure her into coming. He'd thought they'd have a chance to talk, to work things out like two adults. But Cory had set aside the iPod and been a chatterbox the whole way. Never even napped as the surrounding landscape stretched out before them and the terrain took on a more rugged, less populated look. Conversation had been reduced to the superficial to accommodate his presence.

Up ahead he saw the turnoff to his family's Colby Ranch. "This is it."

Cory all but bounced in his seat as they exited the highway and drove under the arch of an interlocking trio of Cs, then headed down the tree-lined, half-mile-long road leading to the main house.

He cut a look at Elise, but she was taking in the view from the passenger side of the vehicle, much as she'd done the entire trip.

He leaned over to slide a hand across hers, startling her into turning toward him. "Everything's going to be fine, Elise. You'll see."

She offered a tight smile, then turned again to the window.

He sank back in the bucket seat. When he'd told Maddie he'd be bringing Elise and Cory with him, she'd squealed in delight. The first words out of her mouth had been "I knew it. I knew it. Right from the beginning when George caught you off guard about having a lady friend back in Fort Worth."

Maddie had been full of nosy questions. She had even put her cell phone on speaker mode so her twin could join in to tease him mercilessly. Violet's whoops still rang in his ears. "Bachelor Boy finally makes his move."

Although he'd protested loudly, he had to admit he'd enjoyed their sisterly jabs. Enjoyed the fleeting moments when he'd believed he and Elise had a future together. Even now, despite present circumstances, the memory amused him.

"What's so funny?"

He glanced at the beautiful woman beside him. "What?"

"You're smiling."

"Sorry."

She motioned impatiently. "There's nothing to be sorry about. I just thought you might want to share."

Share? Tell her about how his sisters had riddled him with questions about their relationship? How for the first time in his life his heart soared that at long last God had led him to the woman of his dreams?

"I was recalling how my sisters enjoy themselves when they're together. They didn't know the other existed until July, but in many ways you'd think they'd always known each other."

"I am looking forward to meeting them. And your twin."

"Yeah? Well, he's a different kind of animal. We're definitely not two peas in a pod. But he's a good guy. I think you'll like him, although I'm sure you'll agree I'm the better-looking one."

His heart warmed when a laugh reached her eyes. That was the first time since this morning at the parking garage, before he got the call about Scott.

"More charming personality, too," he added, desperate to keep those lights dancing in her eyes. Was he pitiful or what? But maybe there was still hope for this weekend. Maybe he could still convince her...of what? That her fears would go away? That he wouldn't die in the line of duty? That he'd give up being a cop?

Even before Elise had come along, he'd given the latter

serious thought during those long, lonely nights on the undercover assignment. Debated the wisdom of a future filled with more long, lonely nights.

He'd seen firsthand how his dad's dedication to a demanding medical career took its toll on relationships. Dad's second wife—Gray's mom—died twenty years ago, but his father never remarried. He had to be lonely. But maybe he'd come to terms that he couldn't devote himself to helping those less fortunate if he had a wife's needs to meet as well.

Gray tightened his fingers on the steering wheel. He loved being a cop. But he loved Elise, too. Maybe that was the difference between his situation and his dad's. His father never found another woman he loved as much as he did medicine. But would his dad sacrifice the demands of a much-loved career to capture the heart of a woman he truly loved?

"There it is!" Her son's excited voice cut through the silence that had once again fallen over the interior of the vehicle. Gray hadn't said much during the drive westward. He'd been lost in thought, only joining in occasionally on back-and-forth conversation with Cory, pointing out various landmarks and answering the city boy's multitude of questions.

How had Cory gotten to be such an urban child, anyway? She certainly hadn't been when growing up in Arizona. The freedom of small-town Canyon Springs was an experience she wouldn't trade for the world. Maybe she'd been wrong to keep herself apart from it these past years. To keep Cory apart from it.

"It's beautiful," Elise whispered as she gazed at the main house nestled among a stand of oaks, a few of the surrounding bushes already taking on a golden autumn cast. The two-story brick structure sprawled comfortably under the warm glow of the midday sun.

Grayson had described the Colby Ranch to her a few nights ago, but nothing prepared her for the stretches of cultivated fields, grasslands dotted with white-faced Herefords, and the stately home gracing the property. All of it had been inherited from the original owner by Grayson's birth mother, Belle. This is where his two siblings had grown up. How strange it all must seem to him.

"I thought it would be a bunk house." Cory sounded disappointed. "Like in the Westerns."

Gray glanced at him in the mirror. "There are older houses scattered around the property that are more what you're thinking of, bud. Original buildings. In fact, my brother Jack is remodeling one of them."

"Look! Horses! Don't forget, Mom, Officer Grayson says I can ride one."

"I haven't forgotten, and I'm sure you'll get to. But when we get out up here, don't go running off. Stick close to me or Grayson. You understand?"

She could envision him crawling under a fence and getting snagged on the barbed wire or knocked over by a too-eager equine checking him out. Stepped on by a cow.

When Grayson shut off the engine, the stillness of their surroundings permeated the cab of the SUV. Dry leaves rustled faintly overhead. No signs or sounds of life except for the distant low of cattle.

"It's quiet here," she whispered, noticing that even Cory sat motionless, head tilted, listening. "I guess I've been living in the city too long. Almost eerie, isn't it?"

"I guess so, now that you mention it." Gray's voice came soft as well, as if reluctant to break the hush that penetrated her very pores, seeping inside her.

"Smells dry, too."

He nodded. "Long-term drought has hit this area hard."

A dog barking broke the quiet, followed by the rattle of a screen door as two auburn-haired young women appeared on the front porch. One dressed in faded jeans, T-shirt and boots had her hair pulled into a perky ponytail. The other, hair caressing her shoulders, looked polished in a crisp cotton camp shirt, designer-fit jeans and tennis shoes.

"Violet has a ponytail and Maddie's the other one." Gray glanced toward Elise, as if gauging if she was ready for this encounter. What had he told his sisters about her? How did they feel about her arrival on their doorstep at such a tumultuous family time?

"They're cute."

He smiled. "They are at that. And, uh, don't put a whole lot of stock in anything they tell you about me, okay? They like to tease. Exaggerate."

Despite his words of caution, his eyes were bright with anticipation as he climbed out of the SUV seconds before his sisters pounced on him, enveloping him in hugs. Elise couldn't help but smile as he returned their exuberant welcome.

When Maddie disengaged herself, she motioned to the vehicle. "Let's see 'em, Gray. You gonna keep 'em cooped up in there all weekend?"

A grinning Cory was already climbing out and readily fell into a group hug as if he'd always belonged there. Elise opened her own door. *Please, Lord, be with me.*

Violet, eyes appraising curiously, embraced her when she joined them. "Welcome to the Colby Ranch. We're so happy to have you here."

Maddie gave her a hug, too. "That's right. It's not every day our big bro brings home a lady friend for us to check out. Looks like you've done all right for yourself, Grayson."

His ears reddened, and once again Elise regretted coming. Obviously his sisters read something into her visit that could only hurt him.

Maddie leaned in with a conspiratorial stage whisper. "Wait till I tell you about the first time he brought a gal home to meet the family. Better than any TV comedy."

Violet clapped her hands. "Oooh, I want to hear this, too."

Grayson chuckled, not looking too worried, but nevertheless he held up a hand. "I think that can wait, ladies. Why don't we unload the luggage and get our guests inside. It was a long drive, and I'm sure they're both tired."

Cory folded his arms. "I'm not tired. I'm ready to pet a cow and ride a horse."

They all laughed and Violet put an arm around his shoulder. "I promise you'll get to do all those things and more. But Grayson's right, let's get you both settled in."

Maddie followed him to the back of the SUV and snagged his clothes bag. "Violet and I took an extended lunch hour, but have to get back to town for our jobs. We'll have a nice long visit at supper tonight." She glanced in Elise's direction, her eyes sparkling mischievously. "And we expect *you* to fill us in on all the details Gray's withheld about how you two met. First kiss and all that. You know, the juicy stuff."

Elise's empathetic gaze met Gray's cheerless one. Letting him talk her into coming was a mistake.

A big one.

Chapter Seventeen

"She's beautiful, Gray. Sweet, too." Maddie had pulled him into the kitchen while Violet showed Elise and Cory to the room they'd share. "And what a darling kid. Don't wait too long to pop the question. I think this one is a keeper."

He stared out the window at the back patio, the house's U-shaped wings flanking it on three sides. Peaceful, with potted flowers providing bright, welcoming spots of color.

"I thought so, too—yesterday. But things took an unexpected turn since I last talked to you. It's the cop thing again."

"From what you said the other night, wasn't she getting used to the idea?"

"It blew up this morning as we were ready to leave. I got a call that a fellow officer, a friend Elise had met, got caught in the crossfire of a domestic disturbance."

"Will he be okay?"

Scott's situation weighing heavily, he turned to his sister. "Don't know yet. He's in critical condition."

"I'm sorry to hear that, Gray. I guess the news hit too close to home for Elise."

"Yeah. The past few days she seemed to be getting more comfortable with me being a cop. The tension between us eased. The future looked promising." He scuffed a toe at the floor. "But after the call, it was a different story. She refused to come to Grasslands for the weekend, saying she couldn't deal with living in daily fear again."

Maddie approached him, a confident lift to her chin. "She can't have irrevocably concluded you're not the man for her. She still came."

"Against her will. I didn't play fair, using the prospect of disappointing Cory as the tool of persuasion."

The hope in her eyes extinguished. "So you're both here this weekend, but essentially—"

"We're not together."

Maddie slipped her arms around his middle for a quick hug. "I thought for sure—"

"Yeah, well. That's the way it goes. Could you get word to Violet? Jack? You know, to knock off the teasing? It will make things awkward."

"Of course." Maddie cast him a sympathetic look. "She may still change her mind. I have every confidence you and that charm of yours will win her back."

He gave her a grateful smile, but shook his head. "Don't count on it. I think only one thing would make her reconsider…"

"You mean if you weren't a policeman." She studied him with troubled eyes. "Could you do that? Give up law enforcement?"

"I honestly don't know. It's not like I haven't given it considerable thought since Jenna made it clear she wanted no part of life with a lawman."

Maddie scoffed. "Jenna didn't deserve you. Maybe Elise doesn't, either."

"Is it realistic, though, to think I can be a good cop and a strong family man? That's what I keep asking myself. The odds of something happening to me like what happened to Elise's husband are slim." Gray shook his head again. "But is it fair to expect a woman to live each day with the uncertainty? The worry? Fear? To marry a man who's already married to his career?"

"Most women learn to live with ongoing fear for the safety of those they love. I'm already in knots when I know Ty's working around the bulls. I watch Darcy like a hawk when she's off on a pony or waiting for the school bus. That kind of fear comes with the territory called love."

"It's more than that. It's like Elise's fears have her gripped around the throat, immobilizing her. She lost her husband in the line of duty, and my career is a constant reminder of that." He looked at Maddie, silently willing her to understand. "She's a wonderful woman. Beyond my wildest hopes and dreams. How stupid can a guy be if he won't give up the one thing that's standing in the way of a lifetime of happiness?"

"She means that much to you?"

He nodded. "I've never felt this way about a woman before. Like God made her for me and me for her. I'd move heaven and earth to keep Elise and Cory in my life."

Maddie glanced toward the arched doorway leading to the front of the house, listening to Cory's exuberant voice as he hopped down the stairs one at a time and the gentle, calming tone of Elise's response as she followed behind.

Maddie turned to look Gray in the eye, her voice a whisper. "Then I guess…you have your answer, don't you?"

Elise hugged her arms to herself, wishing she'd brought a jacket when she'd escaped the confines of the Colby supper hour and slipped out into the still night air. She'd lingered to help clean off the dining table, but Grayson's sisters and their cook had shooed her out. Just as well. After Cory and Darcy had been sent off to play on the back patio, Grayson delivered the sobering news that his father's wallet had been found. They needed to draw close as a family without the intrusive eyes and ears of a stranger.

To her relief, Cory and Darcy had hit it off immediately,

sharing giggles and secrets. Yet another regret—that she and Duke hadn't had another child a few years after Cory so he'd have a built-in playmate. But could she have handled two little ones on her own? She was barely managing one, as was evidenced in Cory's issues at school. At least those had eased somewhat after Grayson had come along, after he'd gotten them out of the neighborhood that had caused her an anxiety which transmitted itself to Cory.

She eased down on the porch's top step.

Grayson.

Lord, what were You thinking when You brought such an amazing man into my life?

She'd hurt him. Her roller-coaster emotional upheavals were now impacting him as much as they did her and Cory. As badly as she ached inside tonight, she knew he ached even more.

Billie Jean warned her he was falling in love with her, but she'd been so tangled in her own misgivings she hadn't given it as much thought as she should have. Caught up in insecurity, she hadn't been willing to acknowledge the many things he did for her and Cory were confirmation of a heart laying itself open in hope of its love being accepted—and returned.

She loved him, too.

But it was better to end things now rather than months or years later. It wasn't fair for him to bear the burden of her fears. It hadn't been easy on Duke. She could look back now and realize why at times he grouchily voiced that he found her clingy. Suffocating even. Always in need of reassurance. Over time that would wear on a man. On a relationship.

"Elise? What are you doing out here?"

She turned at the sound of Grayson's voice as he stepped out on the porch with her. He snagged a small quilt from the back of a rocker and draped it around her shoulders.

"Thanks." She snuggled into its welcoming warmth. "I'm just stargazing."

He settled in beside her, keeping a marked distance between them as if aware that her instincts might urge her to bolt.

"Beautiful night for it."

"Your family's ranch is beautiful, too."

"Wait until you see the rest of it." The quiet eagerness in his voice pricked her conscience. He already loved this place and now her presence here would always shadow his memories of it. "I think Maddie and Violet have a full-fledged tour planned. I'd like to take you into Grasslands and show you around there, too."

"Please don't feel you have to spend time with me while I'm here. We both know I came because of Cory."

He leaned in toward her. "I want you to know, Elise, that I've been real careful about making promises to Cory, not being stupid like I was with Michael."

"You believed you'd be there to fulfill every one of them. It's not your fault his mother didn't see things the way you did."

He shifted restlessly. "I should have recognized the way I felt about Michael far exceeded the depth of my commitment to his mother. She was right to call it off. But I wish she'd have allowed me to gradually wean Michael away, for both our sakes."

"Is that what you want to do with Cory? Gradually ease out of his life?"

He propped his elbows on his knees and lowered his head into his hands. "I don't want to talk about this, Elise."

"We need to."

"I know we haven't known each other long." He lifted his head to gaze at her in the dim light, his eyes filled with pain and his voice husky. "But I've already come to—"

"Don't say it, Grayson. It will make it harder for both of us."

"I don't see how that's possible, unless you don't care for me the way I care for you."

But I do! I love you! her heart cried out, but the words didn't reach her lips. When she tried to imagine a life with him, her mind would flash to the night she'd clung to Duke's still-warm, unresponsive hand, begging him to hear her voice, to open his eyes. This morning, when the call of an officer's injury came in, Grayson's face had superimposed over Duke's in that dark, emotionally raw scene of her imagination. A warning.

"I do care." She kept her voice even. "It's because I care that I'm making a decision to end things now. I'm sorry I've hurt you. It wasn't my intention." If only she could go back in time and never pick up the phone that night to call him, to beg him to spend time with her son. "Now, about Cory—"

Gray's warm, strong hand grasped hers. "No, it's not about Cory. This is about us, Elise. You and me. You can't deny what's been growing between us."

"I'm not denying it. I'm facing the realities of it. Long-term, I'm not what you need."

A disbelieving scoff escaped his lips. "Shouldn't I be the judge of that?"

"You're seeing things in me that will never be there. Things you need. Encouragement. Support. A woman who is strong enough to let you be you and allow you to do what you need to do." For a long moment she squeezed her eyes shut, wishing she could be that woman. "You need a woman who won't hold you back because she's a basket case of irrational fears. A woman who has an unwavering faith and won't demand more from you than you can give."

"You're stronger than you think you are."

"I'm not." She pulled her hand free and slipped the quilt from her shoulders. Dropped it into his outstretched hand as she rose to her feet. "I'm sorry. I want to be. But I'm not."

"What if…" As he gazed up at her, a sudden brightness

lit his eyes. But he hesitated as though debating the wisdom of what he was about to say. Seeing him struggling within piqued her bleak hopes. How she longed for answers. For guidance. For a way to free herself of the fears that bound her.

"What if what?" she prompted.

He shook his head slowly, as though defeated. "Nothing."

Disappointed, she turned away. "Good night, Grayson."

"Heard from Patty Earl again." Jack grimaced as he pushed back from the lunch table and gave Gray a significant look. "It's your turn to take her next call, bro."

"Thank you kindly, but I'll pass." He glanced at Elise, who sat quietly across from him, Cory and Darcy having already gone on a pony ride with Jack's fiancée, Keira. She gave a slight nod to acknowledge she remembered what he'd told her about Patty and Joe Earl—and the unsavory possibility that Joe could be his biological father. "But what's up with the phone calls? I thought she as much as slammed the door in your face the last time you tried to see her. Said she wasn't answering any more questions."

"She's singing a somewhat different tune now." Jack's lip curled in disgust. "Claiming she understands what a shock the truth of my paternity had to be. Said it almost took her breath away how I favor her late husband and that's why she refused to see me. Said I don't look a thing like Brian Wallace."

"Of course you don't." Violet poured herself another glass of iced tea. "You look like Mom, just like the rest of us. What else did she say?"

"Oh, just that had the Wallaces not up and moved away when the kids were small, her husband would have seen to it that his boys got a chance to know him. She now has a sudden hankerin' to spend time with Joe's boys."

Gray grunted. He still wasn't buying this Joe Earl business.

"Yeah, right." Maddie made a face. "I bet she started seeing dollar signs once she did some snooping and learned about the ranch. What if she shows up on our doorstep?"

Gray leaned back in his chair, taking in the dismal expressions on the faces of his siblings. There was only one way to nip this Patty Earl business in the bud, but dare he voice it? His gaze again connected with that of Elise, who communicated silently that she knew what he was thinking. What he was about to say. And approved.

Why couldn't Elise see they belonged together? And why hadn't he been able to get those words out last night to tell her he'd be willing to quit the force?

Jack rose from the table, but Gray motioned him to again be seated. Then he shot another look in Elise's direction for moral support. "I'd like to address something we've likely all batted around in our heads for some time, but nobody's had the gumption to bring up."

All eyes in the room riveted on Gray.

"This Joe Earl business could be settled with a simple DNA test."

Not surprisingly, no one gasped as if the idea hadn't occurred to them. No dirty looks were thrown his way. As he'd suspected, it had been the elephant in the room.

Jack folded his arms on the table. "So let's talk about it."

"But what if…" Maddie looked from one brother to the other. "What if it turns out Dad isn't your biological father?"

"That's a risk." A risk about which Gray had thought long and hard. He didn't like the sounds of Joe Earl or cotton to the idea of being kin.

"Getting a test seems disrespectful." Violet nibbled her lower lip. "Especially to Mom. Shouldn't we wait to hear it from our parents, Grayson?"

"You're forgetting, Vi." Jack's voice was gentle, but firm. "I point-blank asked Mom who our father is, and she wouldn't tell me."

All of them knew it wasn't easy for Jack to bring that up.

The subsequent argument had led to his mother galloping off to a fall from her horse.

"Jack has a point." Gray nodded toward his brother. "We can't dismiss the fact that neither parent has been truthful with us. There have been too many secrets kept, even when we reached adulthood."

From the looks they gave him, it was obvious the direction their thoughts were heading, even if no one voiced it. What if they didn't find Dad? What if Belle never came out of the coma? It was getting easier to think of her as his mother, but would she ever be Mom?

"So you want us to wait, Violet?" He glanced from sister to sister. "What about you, Maddie?"

Jack leaned forward. "I don't want to wait. Gray and I have the right to a definitive answer. The sooner we know, the better. I want to take a test."

Jack didn't know Brian as the man Grayson knew. While he might be intrigued with the prospect of Brian Wallace as a parent, there were still unanswered questions. Questions that no doubt held him back from the affection and respect Grayson felt for their father. Questions such as why he'd go off and leave a son and daughter to be raised by a struggling single mom. From Jack's perspective, Brian Wallace might be no better than Joe Earl.

"There's no point in us both doing it, Jack. I can send in a sample for analysis. Same DNA."

"Two would be more conclusive," his twin countered. "And I say we open the results together, not on our own. We're family now and what affects one of us affects both of us."

"Violet and I'll want to be there when you find out, too," Maddie insisted. "Don't leave us out. But you realize, don't you, that if you're Joe Earl's sons, we're only half siblings."

Jack's brow furrowed. "Full or half won't change the way I feel about y'all. What do we have to do to make this happen?"

"You're sure?" Gray studied his brother, grateful he wouldn't face the moment of paternity truth alone.

"100 percent."

"Then I'll check on recommended testing facilities. We don't need a fly-by-night operation that could get something wrong. I can have a swab kit sent to you. We take a cell sampling from inside our cheeks. Send those in."

Maddie leaned forward. "How long does it take?"

"Normally within a couple of weeks if it's not for court evidence." Gray paused. "But it will take additional time because we can't give Dad a swab kit. I'll have to go to his place and get a hair sample for analysis. That type of testing will take longer."

He glanced at Violet. "You're awfully quiet over there. Are you on board with this?"

"It still seems like we're casting a shadow on our parents. We're insinuating that Mom cheated on our father."

That had troubled him as well. "People aren't perfect, sis."

"No." Her chin lifted obstinately. "But it's *Mom* we're talking about. I feel like we're betraying her."

Maddie slipped a consoling arm around her sister. "I think Jack and Grayson should do it. Otherwise they'll always wonder, you know, if…if we don't…"

If we don't ever get answers from Brian and Belle.

"Violet?" Gray didn't want to trample on her concerns. This needed to be a unanimous family decision.

After a long moment, she nodded. "I understand why it's important for you and Jack to know the truth. So do it with my blessing."

His gaze once again met that of Elise. Why was he still looking to her, seeking her approval, wanting to please her?

"Okay, then. I'll get the ball rolling."

Chapter Eighteen

"This is where you grew up, Officer Grayson?"

Cory peered out the SUV's window at the brick schoolhouse.

"No, I grew up in Fort Worth and a town called Appleton. But this is a lot like the little town I lived in for a while."

"I like it."

Elise noticed on the drive to Grasslands that Gray directed his conversation entirely to Cory. She didn't join in, certain he would much rather have taken her son to town with him alone to run the errand for Violet. But he'd politely extended the invitation, and she'd jumped at the chance to get away from the ranch this afternoon. Not that everyone wasn't kind to her, but it was every bit as awkward as she'd anticipated it would be. Shortly after her initial welcome, it became apparent that Gray had managed to communicate to his siblings the true state of their relationship. Everyone was polite and friendly to her, but they clearly no longer viewed her as belonging. Jack, in particular, had kept his distance.

She repeatedly found herself returning to her room, stepping out on the porch, walking around the yard or playing with the dog. Cory and his playmate Darcy explored the trappings of a working ranch with Gray and various members of his family. But time hung on her own hands.

She suddenly leaned forward. "Oh, look at that cute house!"

No doubt startled at her delighted cry, Gray slowed the vehicle, searching for what had captured her attention. She pointed to the home on a corner lot. How she'd love to live in an adorable place like that. A fenced-in, white-frame house with a Victorian flavor. Lots of trees. Her geranium would be right at home on that wraparound porch.

And it was for sale.

"You like that?" His eyes held a cautious curiosity. "I noticed it when I was here last time, too."

"You did?"

"Yeah. And Sheriff Cole—George—thinks I should buy it."

She couldn't keep the eagerness from her voice. "Are you going to?"

"It's tempting. Just as nice on the inside as the outside."

She continued to gaze with longing at the house as they slowly passed by. A town like Grasslands would be perfect to raise Cory in. Closer to home, too. Maybe nine hours rather than almost fourteen. She'd only been back once, for Duke's funeral. The talk then had been of her coming home, until she'd learned the extent of her husband's debts. The past two years had been such a blur, focused on keeping food on the table, a roof over their heads, and the family from knowing the truth about Duke.

If Grayson bought this darling house, would he rent it to her? But where would she work in a town this size? She'd done more than her fair share of waitressing back home. Tips were good with a summer crowd flocking to the cool, high elevation region, but leaner in the winter months. It was hard work at any rate and work that wouldn't pay enough to support a single mom and her son. No health insurance either—which was the prime reason she'd jumped at the clinic position in Fort Worth.

"Does he want you to buy it for an investment or because he still wants you to join his department?"

"As a matter of fact, he accosted me early this morning when I came in to the care center to spend time with…my mother." He gave a scoffing laugh. "Kinda rankles that a country cop thinks I should jump at the opportunity. What's there to do here besides cruise around in a cowboy hat trying to look important behind a badge?"

"Sounds to me," Elise put a teasing lilt into her tone, "like that's your pride talking."

His brows lowered, obviously not caring for her candid assessment.

"I'm serious. That's how it comes across." And it did. Like he was looking down on a small-town Podunk community from the lofty heights of a much-lauded city force. She'd come from a small town and knew there was more than enough to keep law enforcement busy. From the brooding look on Gray's face, however, she should have kept her mouth shut.

"There's a church!" Cory leaned forward to point. "Is that where we're going?"

"That it is." Gray pulled into a parking space in front of the steepled building and shut off the engine. Then he reached for a sack in the backseat. "I'll be back in a minute."

"I want to take it in." Cory was already unbuckling his seat belt. "Violet says Sadie is a nice lady. She gives kids candy."

Gray glanced at her. "Is that okay with you?"

She wouldn't let Cory set foot outside the yard and kept a close watch on him even there. But what would it hurt for him to feel some independence? Growing up in Canyon Springs she'd often walked to the grocery store or to Dix's Woodland Warehouse to pick up something for her mother.

City life and her own paranoia had forced her to curb Cory from naturally spreading his wings.

"It's fine with me."

In a flash her son was out the door to take the sack from Gray. But he didn't wildly race to the church as she'd anticipated. Instead he marched along, chin lifted, to make the delivery with as much dignity as a six-year-old could muster.

"I've said it before and I'll say it again." Gray settled himself into his seat. "Cory's a great kid."

He sounded almost as proud as she felt watching her son stride up the walkway and disappear inside the main door.

A smile tugged at Grayson's lips. "I imagine that little guy will get a warmer welcome from Sadie than I did the last time I dropped something off."

"Sadie. The church secretary that Maddie says has a crush on the pastor?"

"One and the same. From what I hear, though, it may be a mutual attraction, only neither can get up the courage to make a first move."

"Maybe that's for the best," she said quietly. It would save them a lot of heartache.

She sneaked a glance at Grayson who studied the steering wheel as if it harbored the secrets of the universe. So handsome with his strong profile and sturdy jaw. But more important, he was a man with a heart as big as the Texas he called home. Why had God brought him into her life now? Why not five years from now? Ten? When she'd have had time to work through the fears that haunted her, the nightmares replaying in her sleep.

Only yesterday morning she'd awakened with a sense of peace that God was leading her into something so amazing she could never in her wildest dreams imagine it. But one phone call announcing a police officer's life-threatening injuries and her world had fallen apart. She hated being this way. Hated how her crippling fears affected her son. How they had hurt Grayson. Why couldn't he have been a grocer or insurance salesman?

But, unfortunately for her, he was born and bred to be a lawman.

"So…you don't think there can be happily-ever-afters, Elise?" Gray spoke softly as he gazed through the windshield at the picturesque church, Elise's take on Sadie and the pastor's romance weighing on his heart.

"Maybe for some."

"But not for us?"

"Grayson, let's not discuss this. Please." She fiddled with the zipper on her lightweight jacket. "I'm sorry my being here is making things awkward for you with your family. It was clear from Maddie and Violet's welcome yesterday that they'd formed preconceptions about our relationship."

"That's my fault." He continued to stare out the window. "I'd gotten ahead of myself."

"I'm sorry."

He glanced toward her, only to catch her eye and see her quickly turn away. She was beautiful this morning, with her glossy hair braided down her back. Had she slept any better than he had? Must have. She sure didn't look like he felt after a night of tossing and turning.

He'd given leaving the force a lot of thought. Assuming she'd agree to have him if he wasn't a cop, getting up the guts to say goodbye to police work was all that stood between him and the woman of his dreams. Just as when Maddie had voiced the option yesterday, it sounded so simple. Quit. Get married. Live happily ever after.

But how would he support her and Cory? Provide a home? He couldn't tend to cattle and crops like his brother did.

Cops and crooks. That's all he knew anything about.

A light touch to his arm brought him back to the present.

"I know it wasn't easy to bring up the subject of DNA testing at lunch today."

A muscle in his jaw tightened. "It had to be done."

"It took a lot of courage, especially since I know you share Violet's concerns about prying into your parents' past."

He cast her a bleak look. "I have to admit I don't look forward to looking my dad in the eye and telling him I suspected my birth mother—his wife—had messed around with some other guy. That I concluded he might not be my dad. That's going to hurt him. Badly."

"But you *don't* think that." Her tone held a confident ring. "I've sensed all along that deep down you believe Brian Wallace is your father."

He nodded, the reassurance in her words warming him.

"Can't you see, Gray? With that Earl woman determined to worm her way into your family's midst, what choice do you have but to resort to testing? Not long ago, a family wouldn't have this means to disprove the claims she's making. You need to take advantage of it, if only for your peace of mind."

"You're right. But she seems so sure of herself."

"That doesn't make the story truth. Her husband could have lied to her."

"That's what makes this situation even worse. Joe Earl. He didn't amount to much, from what we're hearing. He's nobody whose blood I'd be proud to have flowing through my veins."

"You are who *you* are, Grayson, not what someone else chose to make of his life. But doesn't who he is make it all the more plausible that he'd lied to his wife? Why he would lie is immaterial. Liars habitually lie, not caring who they hurt."

"True. But she claims when Dad found out his girlfriend— my birth mother—was pregnant, he took responsibility and married her. Then he eventually found out she'd stuck him with Joe Earl's sons because Dad was set to inherit a substantial sum of money from his grandmother." Gray glanced at

Elise. "That would be my great-grandmother, who'd raised Dad. She died when I was small, so I don't remember her. But as much as I don't like the possibility that Joe Earl is my biological father, it might explain a lot about what split our folks up."

"Or not."

"But can't you see why, if it is the truth, Dad may have buried himself in his work all these years? He could have been trying not to think about the betrayal. The divorce. Being stuck raising a boy who belonged to some scuzzy guy who'd gotten his girlfriend pregnant."

Elise gripped his arm. "Gray. Stop. Don't speculate like this. You may not receive them overnight, but I have every confidence you'll get answers to your questions."

He let out a gust of pent-up breath and cast her a bleak smile. "But do I really want them?"

"Wallace!"

A loud rapping came at the driver's-side window. Startled, Gray turned to see the sheriff, his placid, easygoing demeanor a thing of the past.

"Get on out of there. We've got us a situation. Man holding his kids hostage at the old Franklin place. I got clearance to recruit anyone with a badge."

Hands shaking but winning the battle against tears for Cory's sake, Elise steered the SUV down the Colby Ranch road.

Oh, God, please protect him. Protect those children.

"Officer Grayson's a policeman here, too?" Cory gazed out the window at the countryside rolling by. "Cool."

"Like I said, he's helping today." Thank goodness Cory had been inside the church when Grayson retrieved his gun and joined the sheriff in his official vehicle.

Please, God. Please.

Once back at the house, she ushered Cory off to the kitchen to join Darcy and the housekeeper, Lupita, who often watched over her. Then she hurried through the downstairs rooms to seek out…who? Was anyone else at home midafternoon? Jack and Ty would be off doing whatever it is men did on a ranch. Keira would be tending to that ailing cow she'd heard mentioned at lunchtime. Violet was probably at the produce market in town.

Maddie. Maybe Grayson's sister was home. Could that have been her vehicle parked in the shade of the pecan tree off to the side of the house?

"Maddie!" She took the stairs two at a time. Rounded the landing and headed upward to the second floor. "Ma—"

She ran right into her as Maddie stepped out of a bedroom door. Eyes filled with alarm, Grayson's sister grasped her arms. "Hey, take it easy. What's wrong? Is Cory okay?"

Nodding, Elise attempted to draw in a steadying lungful of air. "It's—there's a—"

Maddie led her into the adjoining room and directed her to sit on the bed. "Here. Catch your breath."

"I'm sorry. I'm just—" She dropped to the cushiony softness and held out her hands to show how they were shaking. "There's a hostage situation. The sheriff dragged Grayson into it."

"Whoa. Slow down. A hostage situation? In Grasslands?"

"Some man's holding his kids at gunpoint." Elise reached out to grasp Maddie's hand. "Grayson and I were at the church when the sheriff all but hauled him out of his SUV. They took off in the county vehicle."

"So you drove yourself back out here? Where's Cory?"

"Downstairs with Darcy and Lupita." Elise took another steadying breath. "I don't know what I'll do if anything happens to Grayson."

Maddie crouched before her, holding her hand in a reassuring grip. "Now, let's not talk like that. Grayson's not going to take any crazy chances. He knows his business. He's good at what he does. The best."

"Duke…my husband…was good, too."

Maddie's eyes filled with compassion as she rose to seat herself beside Elise. Drew her close. "Gray's going to be okay."

"I wish I shared your confidence, but—"

"Now, none of that talk. The good Lord's watching over him and those kids."

"You must think I'm a mess." She wiped at her eyes, then gave a half laugh. "And I am. But with all that's going on with your family, you sure don't need me falling apart."

"You're not falling apart. You care for Grayson and you're concerned about him." Maddie gave her a reassuring squeeze. "At times like this, you have to draw down deep, Elise. Deep inside where God's stored up strength you don't even know you have."

"I don't think I have that kind of faith."

"Faith isn't a feeling or a ticket that buys what you need. It's a decision—a matter of the will—to stretch out your hand to receive what's being offered."

"I love your brother." There. She'd said it aloud. But loving didn't change their circumstances, the bad timing for Grayson to come into her life.

His sister gave her an understanding smile. "He's a lovable guy."

"Gray deserves so much more than I can give him. More than I can be for him."

"Nevertheless, he has his heart set on *you,* Elise. I know my brother—he'll do whatever he has to do to win you."

"It will never happen." Elise stared at her hands. "I can't subject Grayson to living with the way I am. Not now. Not ever."

Chapter Nineteen

Gray crouched beside the sheriff, his eyes never leaving the little farmhouse outside of town where twenty-five-year-old Baker Dorz held his two young sons hostage.

A first-grader, like Cory, and a preschooler.

God, please speak to his heart, let him hear what I've been telling him. Get him to let those boys go.

Just two of many officers waiting and watching, Gray and George had been out there for hours, sheltered behind the angled SUV. The last dregs of sunlight now faded into the horizon behind them. A cricket's happy tune seemed out of place.

"I've met him, but don't really know him," George said for the umpteenth time, as if blaming himself for the situation. "They moved in here last summer. His wife says he'd gotten laid off in Lubbock and they lost their house. He found a night-shift position in Cannart, but rent is more affordable in Grasslands. She got a part-time job at the grocery store, so they settled here. Then he lost the new job a few days ago."

"This economy's tough. People have worked hard, done their best and, through no fault of their own, lost everything."

"That seems to be his story. Then he got wind that her ma is trying to talk her into taking the kids and moving back home to Odessa. Add drinkin' to the mix and this is what you wind up with."

Grayson nodded, only half listening, his eyes and ears trained on the house.

George placed a hand on his shoulder. "Sorry about grabbing you off the street and hauling you out here. Shorthanded today."

"No problem."

"At least we have some backup out of sight there, ready to move in." When Gray didn't respond, George cleared his throat. "That pretty little gal you were with. She your girlfriend?"

"Not anymore."

Elise's ashen face filled his memory. How she'd stared blankly as he'd instructed her to drive Cory back to the Colby Ranch in his SUV. Had she found her way okay? Would she make herself sick with worry? Be convinced she'd made the right choice in backing off from a relationship with him?

She'd grasped his arm as he'd exited the vehicle, her eyes begging him not to go. How he'd longed to linger. To reassure her. But kids were in danger. No time to waste. Gray could only lean in to graze her smooth cheek with a quick kiss, knowing he was responsible for the anguish reflected in her eyes.

What kind of man did that to the woman he loved?

The sheriff nodded toward the darkened house. "I think Dorz has been listenin' to you, Wallace. You make a lot of sense."

"Maybe. It's awfully quiet in there. He could be plotting his big finale."

"You've done this before, haven't you? This talkin' sense into someone who ain't sensible."

A muscle twitched in his jaw. "Once."

"Are you one of those cops who talks people off ledges for a living?"

"No. I happened to be first on the scene to make contact. They kept me feeding him the negotiator's verbiage because he refused to talk to anyone but me."

George cut him a guarded look. "How'd it turn out?"

"He let his girlfriend go." Gray's throat tightened. "Then shot himself before we could get to him."

"You think this fella will plug his kids? Come out shootin'? Try to take out some of us before he turns the gun on himself?"

"You never know, George. I pray to God he won't."

Elise stared at the clock in the den. Barely seven-fifteen on Sunday morning. Still dark.

And still no word from Grayson.

Having finally stopped pretending to sleep, she'd showered and dressed hours ago. Come downstairs and poured herself a bowl of cereal. It sat on the coffee table before her, untouched.

She'd prayed all night for Grayson's safety. For those children. For their father who'd become so distraught, so hopeless, he wasn't thinking straight. Did fear grip him as it did her at times? Did he once have a faith in the Creator of the universe that tragic events had shattered?

Faith. She'd always thought of herself as a woman of faith. She'd turned her life over to God as a teenager. Always looked to Him in times of trouble. But could someone who professed to have faith in God be such a mess inside? After Duke's death, she no longer felt the presence of the faith that had once been such a large part of her life.

But Maddie had said something about faith not being a feeling at all. Nor was it something earned to be exchanged. She said faith was a decision to reach out and receive what God was offering you. Casting your cares on Him, isn't that how she'd once heard it put?

A decision. Was it that simple? No trying to conjure up

feelings you didn't feel. No trying to be good enough to somehow twist God's arm or convince Him you were deserving. Just making a decision to accept what He lovingly offered and trusting that He'd never leave you or forsake you.

"Mom?"

Cory stood in the doorway in his pajamas and robe, rubbing his eyes and blinking as they adjusted to the light. She held out her arms and he shuffled over to her for a hug. She pulled his small, warm body close, ever thankful that the love she and Duke had shared had brought this precious child into the world.

"Mom? Is Officer Grayson back yet?"

She forced a smile. "Not yet, sweetheart. But I imagine he'll be along as soon as he finishes his work."

"Police work."

She nodded.

With a sleepy-eyed gaze, he looked around the room. "Why are you in here? Lupita's in the kitchen."

She'd been drawn to this room, the place where Grayson had slept on a sofa bed Friday night. Somehow she felt closer to him here.

"I didn't want to be in the way of breakfast preparations."

He pointed at the placemat, bowl and spoon on the coffee table. "Is that your breakfast?"

"Kind of soggy, isn't it?"

He jogged his head up and down in agreement as she enveloped him in another hug. He gave a happy sigh and wrapped his arms around her neck. How she loved this little boy.

Over his shoulder she glimpsed a simple wooden frame on the wall, one she hadn't previously noticed. The narrow oak border edged a series of cross-stitched words. Curious, she stood and lifted Cory into her arms. He snuggled in close as she approached the decorative stitch work.

TRUST GOD NOT ONLY FOR YOUR ETERNITY, BUT FOR YOUR TODAY.

A tingling sensation raced up her arms. Is that what she was guilty of? Willing to place faith for eternal life in God's hands—yet living life these past few years, trying to maintain control, because God couldn't be trusted with it?

Shaken, she stared at the simple words.

"Hold on, George." Grayson leaned forward in the passenger seat of the sheriff's vehicle to confirm what he was seeing. "Looks like you won't have to take me all the way out to the ranch after all. That's my SUV right there, over to the side of the church."

"Maybe your little lady dropped it off for you."

"Could be. Won't do me any good, though, unless it's unlocked and the key's in the ignition. Don't know if that's such a hot idea even in a community like Grasslands."

George chuckled as he pulled in beside Gray's vehicle. "You want to check it out before I drive off and leave you here? Don't know about you, but I'm ready for some shut-eye."

Grayson rubbed his stubbly jaw. "And a shave to go with it."

"Maybe a hot breakfast."

"Now you're talking." Grayson reached for the door handle. "Give me a sec, okay?"

"Wallace?"

Grayson paused.

"Thanks for giving us a hand. Things don't always turn out like we'd hope—but you made a difference. We sure could use a man like you in our department."

Grayson nodded as weariness slammed home. The nerve-racking night had wrung him out. By dawn his perspective on rural law enforcement had made an abrupt about-face. Unlike in the city where your duty was to serve and protect the many strangers who crossed your path, in a place like this you guarded the welfare of your neighbors, family and friends. If it weren't for Elise's aversion to men with a badge, he'd take on the job here. Proudly.

But it didn't much matter now. He'd come to a decision. "I appreciate the vote of confidence, George, but—"

Catching movement through the head-high, leafy hedge bordering the street side of the church prayer garden, his breath wedged in his lungs.

Elise.

What was she doing here this early? Sunday school wouldn't start for at least another hour. "I think I see my designated driver, George. Catch you later."

He could hear the SUV pulling away as he skirted the hedge, but his eyes were focused on glimpses of Elise's graceful form through the foliage. She was dressed for church in a jacketed sundress, hair tumbling loose around her shoulders as she strolled through the garden. Paused to examine a crepe myrtle leaf. A rose.

A picture of peace.

He rounded the corner of the hedge and stepped to the trellis-arched garden entrance. Heart pounding, he hesitated, reluctant to invade this haven of flowering beauty—beauty enhanced by the woman who had her back to him, now gazing up at the cloudless sky.

I don't deserve her, God. But here goes.

"Elise."

She whirled at the sound of his voice, uncertainty in her eyes as their gazes met. "The boys...?"

"Safe. He released them shortly before dawn."

"And the man?"

"He put down his gun and came out."

She momentarily closed her eyes, a whispered thank-you on her lips. Her gaze locked with his, she took a hesitant step.

Paused. Then rapidly covered the ground between them to fall into his arms.

It is not good for the man to be alone….

He held her for the longest time, neither of them saying a word as her warmth pressed against him and his cheek brushed the softness of her flowing hair. Elise, his beautiful Elise. If only he could hold her in his arms like this for a lifetime. But had she sought comfort in his arms out of relief that the kids were okay? Or because he'd returned to her safely—and she needed him in her life, too?

Together they listened in silence to Sunday morning awakening around them. The twitter of a robin. A dog in the distance. A car passing on the street. He tightened his unslinged arm around her as he breathed in the garden scents of foliage and flowers—and the sweetness of Elise.

All too soon, she drew slightly away to look up at him, her lovely face and inviting lips only inches from his own. His breath caught. Should he? Is that what she wanted?

As if reading his mind, she took a step back, forcing him to release her. The blush in her cheeks hinted at embarrassment for the public display of affection she'd unthinkingly initiated.

She darted an uncertain look at him. "I—"

"I got some other good news this morning." He couldn't bear to hear her apologize, to tell him the embrace that warmed his heart was intended only as a platonic one. "My friend Scott came through the surgeries. He's going to make it. And his wife just found out she's pregnant."

Elise's eyes brightened with tears as she glanced away, blinking rapidly. "I prayed so hard for him—and her. For that man who took his kids hostage. And…and for you."

For him. Why was that so hard for her to admit? Did she think it would imply more than she could commit to?

"Thank you. It appears you have a hotline to heaven." He gently tilted her face toward him, brushing away a tear that slipped down her cheek, his words soft. "Are you okay? I worried about you last night. About how I took off so abruptly. I know it upset you."

She offered a tentative smile. "I guess that sort of thing goes with cop territory, doesn't it?"

"It does, but…" He continued to gaze down at her, attempting to read her heart, the meaning behind her words. It had taken him a long time to work through things in the stillness of the night. Forgiving his father for withholding family secrets. Coming to terms with the fact that even if Brian Wallace wasn't his biological parent, Dad was still his dad. Weighing the dream of being a policeman against sharing his life with Elise. "If it will make a difference in the way you feel about me, Elise…if I mean enough to you that you'll give me another chance…I'll quit the force."

With a soft gasp, she drew back, uncertainty flickering in her eyes.

"Law enforcement draws me like a magnet." He had to be honest with her. "But it pales against the hope of having you and Cory in my life. I mean, if that's what you'd want, too."

She stared at him as if uncomprehending. "Grayson, do you know what you're saying? You were born to be a police officer."

"You don't think I'm capable of doing anything else? Hey, I can flip burgers with the best of them." He grinned, mimicking holding a spatula and tossing a beef patty aloft.

She didn't laugh.

"But…being a policeman is who you are."

How could he explain it to her? Make her understand that she and Cory were his world now? Or maybe it didn't matter. Maybe she'd used the policeman thing as a smoke screen, camouflaging the fact that she didn't care for him the way he cared for her. She'd used the excuse as a means of letting him down in a way that wasn't such a personal rejection. Not saying, "I don't love you," but rather, "I can't deal with policemen."

He drew a resolute breath.

"Law enforcement is just one facet of who I am. It's what I've done for a living. But I want to be so much more than that. I want to be a husband. A father. An active member of a community where people recognize each other on the street. I've seen too many strained relationships in the department. Too many divorces. Broken families. As you already know from losing Duke, life is too short not to live it to the full."

"But...what will you do if you quit, Gray? I mean—"

Another attempt to deflect his request for a second chance? "I have a criminal justice degree and five years of law enforcement experience. That might be useful in a number of law-related jobs that don't involve guns."

She nibbled her lower lip, her gaze still troubled. "You've given this considerable thought, haven't you?"

"I'm ready to turn in my badge, move to Grasslands and buy that little house that's for sale." He cupped her face in his hand, longing for the day he'd be free of the sling and could hold her the way he really wanted to. "That is, if it will make a difference...for us."

Her eyes filled with doubt. "But giving up law enforcement?"

There was only one way to settle this, and that meant placing his heart at her feet.

"I don't know how you feel about me. Maybe, police officer or not, I'm not the man you're looking for." His eyes never wavered from hers. "But...I love you, Elise. The kind of love that asks, will you marry me?"

For an agonizingly long moment she stared at him, her mind no doubt racing to weigh the pros and cons of hooking up with a guy like him. Or coming up with ways to let him down easily.

Please, God? I'll treasure her for the rest of my life.

I promise.

Her gaze flickered anxiously to his. "Oh, Grayson, I love you, too…but—"

An invisible boulder slammed into his midsection. Yes, she loved him, but like a brother. A friend.

"But what?" he said, barely choking out the words.

"I—I'm sorry…but I can't marry you." Her words came breathlessly. "I mean, I can't marry you unless…"

Hope sparked again. There was nothing he wouldn't do, no mountain he wouldn't climb for the woman standing before him. "Anything, Elise. Name it."

"I can't marry you—" she licked her lips "—unless you pursue the deputy sheriff position you told me about."

He shook his head. Had he heard her right?

"You're a fine police officer, Grayson." Her chin rose slightly in that stubborn tilt he was already too familiar with. "I refuse to take that away from you."

"But I thought— I mean, I don't want you living the rest of your life being afraid I'll come to the same end as your husband. That's no way to live."

She shook her head. "No, it hasn't been a good way to live these past two years. But that's my own fault."

His gaze probed hers.

"You see, Gray, I've come to realize over the past few days that getting involved with another police officer isn't the source of my fear. Needing to be in control of everything around me isn't the origin of my unbending pride. Those are mere symptoms."

He tilted his head, listening intently.

"Fear and misplaced pride." A knowing gleam lit her eyes. "Those are flashing red warning lights I was too blind to see. Warnings that those symptoms are rooted in a lack of trust."

"In me?"

A tender smile lifted the corners of her mouth.

"No. In God." She reached for his hand and wove her

fingers between his. "Just as Cory has done, I've too long harbored deep anger over the loss of Duke. Over his poor choices. I was angry with him—with God. I convinced myself that I alone could control my world, prevent bad things from happening to myself and the people I love. But this morning…"

His gaze intensified.

"I've come to realize that by not trusting God, I'm cutting myself off from a future with one of the most wonderful men I've ever known."

Encouraged, he hiked an expectant brow. "That's me, I hope."

Her shy nod warmed his heart. "I love you, Grayson Wallace. And yes, I will marry you—but only if it means I'll become Mrs. Deputy Grayson Wallace."

"You're sure?"

"I've never been more certain of anything."

He stared down at their clasped hands, then met her gaze with soft words of his own. "I think we can arrange that."

"Don't be deceived." She hurried on, as though a caution was in order. "I can't promise I'll never be afraid. That I won't worry about you. But from this day forward, I'm deciding to trust God not only for my eternity, but for my today."

He drew her into his arms, casting a furtive glance around the still-empty garden. Then a grin he could no longer restrain surfaced. "Don't you think, soon-to-be Mrs. Deputy Grayson Wallace, that an occasion like this calls for something of a celebratory nature?"

Her gaze held his, a mixture of anticipation and curiosity.

"Like maybe—" he wiggled his eyebrows "—a little of that long-overdue kissing?"

With a sigh of delight, Elise slipped her arms around his neck. "I do. I do. I do."

Epilogue

"So your little brother doesn't have any idea whatsoever what he's walking into?" Elise looked doubtfully from Grayson to Maddie and back again.

As they strolled through the Dallas-Fort Worth International Airport terminal where Marine Sergeant Carter Wallace was scheduled to land within the hour, overhead speakers blared announcements of incoming and outgoing flights. Tunnel-visioned travelers marched rapidly around them, hoisting laptop bags and dragging suitcases on wheels, intent on getting through security and catching their flights.

Brother and sister shook their heads in unison in response to her question.

"I can see why you didn't want to tell him that your father's missing—you wouldn't want to distract him while he was overseas. But you haven't told him the happy news about two sets of twins? A ranch? Four siblings engaged to be married?"

They shook their heads again.

"Oh, boy." Nobody had talked about it much, but she'd gotten the impression that Carter was exasperatingly independent—a loner from the get-go—and he, Grayson and

Maddie had never been close. She'd kind of hoped that was an exaggeration. Apparently not.

"Hey, Mom! Look! Another one." Cory stood a few feet away, nose all but pressed against the glass as he watched a passenger jet rapidly rise from the ground to kiss the gray November sky. "I want to be a pilot when I grow up."

Grayson and Elise exchanged an amused glance. Even with Grayson interviewing for the deputy sheriff opening—and as good as promised the position—Cory's cop obsession had diminished noticeably over the past week. He talked less and less about being a hero, getting the bad guys, or pursuing a career in law enforcement. In fact, yesterday he'd announced he planned to be a rancher like his soon-to-be Uncle Jack and Uncle Ty. Now the big airlines had captured his ever-active imagination.

"What did I tell you, Elise?" Grayson grinned. "Nothing to worry about."

"Think you're so smart, don't you?"

"Know it." He took a step closer and captured her hand. Drew it to his lips for a lingering caress, his gaze burning into hers.

A woman could get used to this kind of attention.

"All right. That's enough." Maddie made a time-out gesture.

"I don't know, Maddie..." Grayson nodded toward knots of couples outside security saying tearful goodbyes between passionate kisses. "Who's to say those people are actually going anyplace. Maybe they're taking advantage of the setting."

Elise tugged playfully on his hand, casting him a coy glance. "Is that a game you'd like to play, Officer Wallace?"

He moved in closer, his eyes flickering suggestively to her lips. "I could be persuaded."

"Oh, no you don't." Maddie latched on to Grayson's arm

and tugged. "Not when Ty can't be here so I can join in on the fun. So knock it off."

Grayson squeezed Elise's hand and winked.

"How will I know who Uncle Carter is?" Dancing around them, Cory paused to pry their hands apart, taking one in each of his own. "Does he know you're going to be my other dad?"

"You'll know him because he's a big ugly dude. Probably in fatigues."

Maddie elbowed her brother. "Oh, Gray."

Cory's face crinkled. "What's *fat geese?*"

Gray chuckled as he gazed with love at the boy soon to be his son, and a sense of wonderment filled Elise. Had she known this amazing man only four weeks? How had God worked such a miracle in such a short time?

"*Fuh-teegs,* buddy. Work clothes worn in the military. And no, he doesn't know about you. I've saved you for a surprise."

Cory brightened. "I'm a surprise for Uncle Carter? Do I get to jump out of a box or something?"

Elise smiled down at him. He'd obviously seen the newscasts covering homecoming soldiers—but usually it was the soldiers who surprised their kids like that, not the other way around.

"I don't have any boxes." Gray frowned thoughtfully. "But you could ride on my shoulders so you'll be the first one he sees."

"Can I?"

Gray turned to reach for him, but Elise stayed him with her hand. "Your shoulder, Gray. Not a good idea."

He grimaced. "Oh, right. Keep forgetting now that I'm free of the sling and scheduled to return to work."

Disappointment colored Cory's expression, but Grayson wasn't to be deterred.

"Wait right here. I have a better idea."

"Where's he going, Mom?"

She and Maddie shared an "it beats me" smile, then her future sister-in-law moved away to a bank of overhead monitors to check incoming flights.

What must have seemed like an interminable amount of time to a six-year-old was actually an amazingly short mission. A wide grin spread across Gray's handsome face, he wove toward them through the crowds, an oversize shopping bag clasped in his fist.

"Here he comes, Mom!"

When he reached them, Gray knelt to open the bag as her—*their*—son crowded in. In no time flat, he got Cory into a blue-and-white T-shirt emblazoned with the Dallas Cowboys official logo. Then pulled a kid-size white cowboy hat from the bag and popped it onto his head.

"Carter's sure to notice you in this. He's a die-hard Dallas Cowboys fan."

"Cool." Cory hugged him, then Grayson glanced at his watch. "Guess we'd better get going if we want to be there when he disembarks."

Cory's forehead wrinkled as he looked up at her. "What's… that bark thing?"

"Gets off the plane." Her eyes smiled into Grayson's and she again marveled at the love reflected in his eyes.

Thank you, Lord.

Cory reached for her hand. Then Gray's. And together with Maddie they headed through the terminal.

As a family.

* * * * *

Dear Reader,

Thank you for joining me for book #4 of the Texas Twins series! It's been a delight to read the first three written by Marta Perry, Barbara McMahon and Arlene James. I feel privileged to have been asked to join such talented writers in bringing these interwoven stories to life.

In watching Grayson and Elise's story unfold, I've seen how God works through circumstances and an inner nudging to open our eyes and change our hearts. Growing up in God—how important that is if we're to learn how to trust Him and, by an act of the will, stretch out our hand of faith to receive what He wants to give us. Not only eternal life with Him through his son Jesus, but love, joy, hope and peace in the here and now. Against all odds, He brought Grayson and Elise all that and more.

And now, like you, I can hardly wait to read the final two books written by Kathryn Springer and Jillian Hart!

I love to hear from readers, so please contact me via email at glynna@glynnakaye.com or Love Inspired Books, 233 Broadway, Suite 1001, New York, NY 10279. Also check out my website www.glynnakaye.com—and stop in at www.seekerville.net and www.loveinspiredauthors.com.

Thank you again for spending time with Grayson, Elise and Cory. If you enjoyed *Look-Alike Lawman,* be sure to visit Elise's hometown of Canyon Springs, Arizona, in my other books!

Glynna

Questions for Discussion

1. Elise has kept her husband's secret for two years, isolating herself from family and friends in order to do so. Do you think it was a wise decision? Why or why not? What part does blaming herself for the choices her husband made play in her decision-making? Have you ever had to deal with a similar situation? What decisions did you make and what were the consequences?

2. Grayson's reeling from the reality that he and his sister Maddie each have a twin. How would you feel if today you discovered you had a twin from whom you'd been separated when you were small? Happy? Angry? Would you want to meet them immediately or need time to come to terms with the situation?

3. Cory and Grayson bond immediately. What kind of impact do you think Gray will have on Cory's life as the little boy grows up? Do you think—as Elise initially did—that Cory would be better off with a stepfather who isn't a policeman? Why or why not?

4. Elise brings her potted pink geranium—all that she has left of her previous garden—to the Fort Worth apartment and places it on the front steps. She takes it with her to Maddie's high-rise apartment—and when she spies a little Victorian house in Grasslands, she immediately thinks it would look right at home on that wraparound porch. What do you think this geranium symbolizes to Elise?

5. Grayson's trying to come to terms with the fact that the woman he thought was his birth mother isn't after all.

He loves his dad, but wonders why his biological mother didn't choose to keep him when she so obviously loves his brother, Jack. What feelings and questions would you struggle with if you suddenly learned you had a parent you never knew existed? Why do you think Brian Wallace kept the existence of Grayson's mother a secret even when Gray became an adult?

6. Gray and Elise both grew up in small towns, at least for part of their childhood. What do you think appeals to them about Grasslands and why? Do you think they'd feel the same about the little community if they'd never before experienced small-town life?

7. Gray doesn't like the idea of being anyone but Brian Wallace's son. He knows DNA testing can provide definitive answers for himself and his brother, but he has a number of concerns about testing. If you were in the same situation, what reservations, if any, might you have? Do you think that he'd have made the same decision if Patty Earl hadn't attempted to intrude on the family?

8. Billie Jean has been a good friend since Elise moved to the rough neighborhood in Fort Worth. How does she help Elise see herself and Grayson more clearly? Why do you think this friendship works even though they come from very different worlds? Do you imagine the friendship will continue through the years? What will it take to keep it alive?

9. Although he's immediately attracted to Elise, Grayson initially has strong reservations about involvement with another woman who has a child. He's haunted by promises he made to another little boy and didn't keep. Do you

feel Grayson broke promises, even if unintentionally? At what point do you sense he's willing to move ahead to give the relationship with Elise a chance? What are the boundaries he's placed on his relationship with Cory? Do you think these limitations would make a difference if things didn't work out for him and Elise?

10. Gray returned from a close-call undercover assignment, determined to build a stronger relationship with his father. What about the close-call do you think triggered that desire? Even though he hasn't had an opportunity to talk to his dad since returning from his assignment, what makes you believe Grayson is coming to better understand the man he believes to be his father?

11. How does Elise gradually come to recognize that her pride issues and chronic fear are symptoms of something far more serious—a failure to trust God? What role do crisis situations play in forcing her to face the truth about herself?

12. Grayson loves being a cop and has a bright future ahead of him in law enforcement. He's come to love Elise, too, but his career and love life aren't meshing, so he's given serious thought to the direction of his professional life. Have you ever had to choose between two "right" things when it appeared impossible to have both? How did you do that? What was the outcome?

13. Elise thinks she's been putting on a good front for her son when she's afraid. What might be a giveaway to Cory that she isn't as strong and fearless as she'd like to think herself? Do you agree with Gray that this is what could be causing Cory's behavioral problems? In

what ways do you believe Cory's behavior will modify as Elise learns to continuously put her trust in God?

14. What do you think it is about the night when Grayson assists the sheriff's department that helps him come to a decision regarding his career? Was it a good decision or a poor one? Why or why not? Elise makes a decision, as well—how does an act of will to trust rather than operate solely on feelings change her situation?

15. Knowing how Cory idolizes his policeman father and how Elise loved Duke, do you think there will come a time when she will tell Cory about his dad's wrong choices and how they impacted his wife and son? If you were Cory's mother, how would you explain the situation to him?